THE HIDDEN WORLD OF
Changers

No. 2: The Emerald Mask

by H. K. Varian

Simon Spotlight

New York   London   Toronto   Sydney   New Delhi

This book is a work of fiction. Any references to historical events, real people, or real places are used fictitiously. Other names, characters, places, and events are products of the author's imagination, and any resemblance to actual events or places or persons, living or dead, is entirely coincidental.

SIMON SPOTLIGHT
An imprint of Simon & Schuster Children's Publishing Division
1230 Avenue of the Americas, New York, New York 10020
This Simon Spotlight edition June 2016
Copyright © 2016 by Simon & Schuster, Inc.
Text by Ellie O'Ryan
Illustrations by Tony Foti
All rights reserved, including the right of reproduction in whole or in part in any form.
SIMON SPOTLIGHT and colophon are registered trademarks of Simon & Schuster, Inc.
For information about special discounts for bulk purchases, please contact Simon & Schuste
Special Sales at 1-866-506-1949 or business@simonandschuster.com.
Designed by Nick Sciacca
The text of this book was set in font.
Manufactured in the United States of America 0516 FFG
10 9 8 7 6 5 4 3 2 1
ISBN 978-1-4814-6620-2 (hc)
ISBN 978-1-4814-6619-6 (pbk)
ISBN 978-1-4814-6621-9 (eBook)
Library of Congress Catalog Card Number 2015945315

Nahual

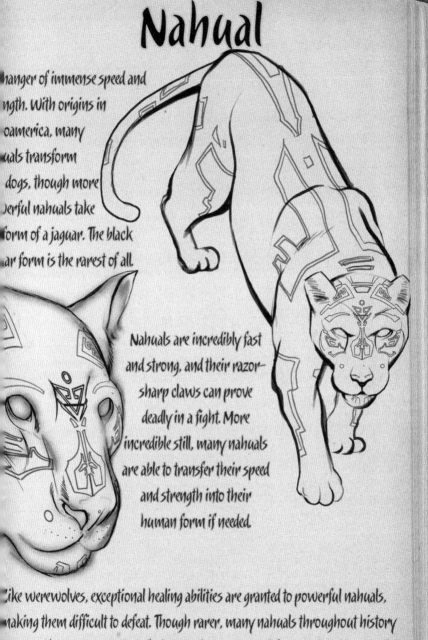

...hanger of immense speed and
...ngth. With origins in
...oamerica, many
...uals transform
... dogs, though more
...erful nahuals take
...orm of a jaguar. The black
...ar form is the rarest of all.

Nahuals are incredibly fast
and strong, and their razor-
sharp claws can prove
deadly in a fight. More
incredible still, many nahuals
are able to transfer their speed
and strength into their
human form if needed.

...ike werewolves, exceptional healing abilities are granted to powerful nahuals,
...aking them difficult to defeat. Though rarer, many nahuals throughout history
...ave been known to spirit walk, leaving their corporeal forms behind to enter the
...houghts and dreams of others. With their myriad abilities and extraordinary
...ighting prowess, the nahual is not a Changer to anger.

PROLOGUE

Run.

It was the only thought on Gabriella Rivera's mind; the thought that played again and again, over and over, as she darted down the soccer field.

Run.

Somewhere, deep down, Gabriella was probably aware of the world beyond the field: the golden autumn sun slicing through a clear, blue sky; the cheerleaders practicing a new routine on the track; the late buses rumbling in the parking lot, waiting to take everyone home from their after-school activities. But in the moment, all Gabriella cared about was:

The goal at the end of the field.

The tattered practice ball at the tip of her foot.

And the pounding of her heart, strong and steady, as she ran at top speed.

Run.

Other players? What other players? Gabriella had left them all in the dust—except for Trisha, who was practicing her goalie skills across the field. A sudden alertness washed over Gabriella as she fixed her eyes on Trisha. Trisha was poised, ready to block any goal Gabriella tried to make. It was totally obvious that Trisha was trying to predict Gabriella's next move. Gabriella could tell from the way Trisha's shoulders were tensed; from the way her eyes followed Gabriella, watching for a sign, a tell ...

No way, T, Gabriella thought. *Not this time.*

An extra burst of speed—Gabriella didn't know exactly how she channeled it, but she had a pretty good idea ...

The thud of her foot making contact with the ball—

Her toes reverberating inside her cleat—

The solid leather ball sailed through the air as free and weightless as the fluff from a dandelion.

I *did that,* Gabriella marveled. I *did it.*

What choice did Trisha have but to drop to the ground, face-first in the grass? Better than a soccer ball to the face, there was no doubt about that.

Time shifted, somehow, and the seconds between the ball tearing through the net and the piercing shriek of Coach Connors's whistle slowed, stretched while Trisha lifted her head and locked eyes with Gabriella.

Something in Trisha's eyes made Gabriella flinch, and the spell was broken. Sound came rushing back: the whistle, the cheers from the rest of their teammates, the voices of kids heading to their buses. All the ordinary noises one would expect to hear at Willow Cove Middle School on a Tuesday afternoon.

"Great work, girls. Excellent practice," Coach Connors was saying. "You play like that on Saturday and the Middletown Marauders don't stand a chance."

Trisha was already lifting herself out of the dirt, but Gabriella reached for her arm anyway.

"Trisha, I am so sorry," Gabriella said as she helped Trisha to her feet. "Are you okay?"

"Sorry? Are you serious?" Trisha asked, ignoring Gabriella's question. "What you did—that move—it was

4

incredible! I've been playing goalie for years, and I have *never* seen anyone score like that. *Ever.* Coach is right. If you play even half that good on Saturday, we're going to win for sure."

Gabriella grinned. "If we win on Saturday, it's because you'll be blocking the goal," she replied. "The Marauders better get ready for a big zero on the scoreboard."

Secretly, Gabriella was relieved Trisha wasn't angry with her. Last month Gabriella had finally cut ties with her popular friends, Daisy Park, Katie Adaire, and Lizbeth Harris. It was tough, and Gabriella still took a lot of flak from them, but the girls on the soccer team were quickly becoming Gabriella's new friends. The best part was that her soccer friends didn't put her down or pressure her to be mean, and that was like a breath of fresh air to Gabriella.

Coach Connors approached them with the ball bag.

"Blew another net, Coach," Trisha reported.

Coach Connors shook his head as he examined the ragged hole where the ball had blasted right through the net. "I can't get mad," he said. "We've never had so many consecutive wins before. The team is on fire this year. But, Gabriella, *try* to take it a little easy on the equipment, would you? I don't know how I'm going to ask for replacements if this keeps up."

"Sorry, Coach," Gabriella said. "I got a little carried away."

"I know," Coach Connors replied. "But save it for Saturday, okay?"

Then he tossed the ball bag toward Trisha; as team captain it was her responsibility to gather all the soccer balls that had been used for drills.

"Here," Gabriella said, reaching for the bag. "Let me help."

"Thanks," Trisha replied. They split up for a while, crisscrossing the field as they gathered several soccer balls. Soon there was just one ball left—the one that Gabriella had kicked through the net. Only hitting the side of the school had stopped it.

"You go," Gabriella said to Trisha. "I know you have a bus to catch. I walk home, so I'm not in a rush."

Trisha glanced over her shoulder at the buses idling in the parking lot. "This is my responsibility," she began.

"And it's my fault the ball is all the way over there," Gabriella said, laughing easily in the sunshine. It felt good—*so good*—to be at the top of her game, to be unstoppable on the field, to have such good friends playing by her side. She couldn't *wait* for Saturday's game.

Then Gabriella noticed she was laughing alone.

"What?" she asked self-consciously as Trisha stared at her. "Is there grass in my hair or something?"

"No," Trisha said slowly. "It's your eyes. They . . ."

"What?" Gabriella repeated, anxiety quivering down her spine.

"It's just . . . They're brown, right?" Trisha asked, peering at Gabriella. "They look brown now, I mean. But on the field . . ."

Gabriella fought the urge to look down; to cover her eyes and sprint away from Trisha. *Act normal*, she ordered herself, which was easier said than done.

"I thought they were yellow!" Trisha continued excitedly. "Like a cat or something! Isn't that weird?"

Gabriella forced herself to laugh. "So weird," she said. "My eyes have always been brown. Maybe the sun was in them or something."

"Yeah," Trisha said. "My mom always says that light plays tricks and stuff."

"Go," Gabriella said. "Get your bus. I'll bring all the equipment back to the gym."

"Thanks, Gabriella," Trisha said. "You really are the best—on the field *and* off!"

Gabriella kept a smile plastered on her face as Trisha jogged past her. She kept smiling as she grabbed the ball and shoved it into the bag with all the others. In the distance she could hear the afternoon buses starting to leave the parking lot. In just minutes the field had practically emptied. It was safe now, Gabriella knew, to drop the act.

She placed her hand on the rough brick wall and exhaled deeply as she stared at the ground. What Trisha didn't know—could never know—was that there had been no trick of the light. She hadn't imagined those golden, glinting cat eyes in Gabriella's face. The truth was that Gabriella was more than a seventh grader at Willow Cove Middle School; she was more than a star soccer player for the Willow Cove Clippers. She was a Changer—a shape-shifter, a *nahual*, a rare and powerful person who could transform from human to jaguar.

And despite all of Gabriella's best efforts to keep her *nahual* side a secret, it had showed itself on the field— in front of everyone.

Chapter 1
A New Threat

The next day Fiona Murphy hoisted her heavy backpack over her shoulder and shuffled out of the cafeteria the moment the bell rang to end lunch. Most other kids were still eating and laughing, balling up their trash and trying to throw it into the garbage can while the cafeteria monitor's back was turned. But Fiona's next class was all the way across school, and she was not the kind of student who got tardies. Ever. And *especially* not when her first big homework assignment of the year, an oral *and* written report, was due.

The report.

A worried frown crossed Fiona's face just thinking

about it. This was the first time in her entire life that she knew, deep down, she was about to get a bad grade. Fiona studied hard for every quiz; she always had her homework neatly completed on time. This report, though, had been impossible. Fiona had done her best, of course. She always did. But even Fiona had to admit that this time, her best wasn't good enough. And that was a very hard thing to face.

It's too late to do anything about it now, Fiona reminded herself. *Better get it over with.*

Soon, Fiona reached the Ancillary Gym, the place where her life had changed forever on the first day of seventh grade. Along with three kids she barely knew—Gabriella Rivera, Darren Smith, and Mack Kimura—Fiona had discovered a secret about herself that even now, even after everything that had happened, was still kind of hard to believe. She was a Changer, part of a magical line of shapeshifters that history had forgotten. Changers hold incredible power and can transform into different creatures from mythology. Fiona had learned she was a *selkie* and could transform into a seal. Darren, an *impundulu*, could become a massive bird and shoot lightning bolts from his hands. Mack was a *kitsune* and could change into a magical fox, just like his grandfather. And Gabriella, a *nahual*, could transform into a powerful black jaguar. In addition to transformations, each one had special powers that they were still learning how to use. Their teacher, Ms. Dorina Therian, was a Changer too—a werewolf, to be precise—and guided them through their powers and intense training every day.

Though Fiona had been the first one to leave the cafeteria, she was the last one to reach the Ancillary Gym. It was like her feet had dragged on purpose, doing everything to delay the moment when she had to give a less-than-perfect presentation. She took a look at the other students, but nobody else seemed even a little concerned. Gabriella and Darren were chatting together on the bench while Mack was sitting on the floor off to the side, furiously sketching in his notebook, surrounded by comic books.

Just then, Gabriella waved her over. "How's your report?" she asked. "I barely finished mine in time."

Fiona smiled—or tried to.

"Too much stuff, right?" Darren asked knowingly. "I swear I could write a whole *book* about *impundulus*. What's the coolest thing you learned about *nahuals*, Gabriella?"

Gabriella looked thoughtful. "I guess I was surprised to learn that *nahuals* can use some of their powers, like superspeed and -strength, in human form," she replied. "I didn't think that was possible."

Darren grinned. "I doubt anybody who's seen you run would be surprised."

The way Gabriella's shoulders stiffened was barely perceptible, but Fiona noticed immediately. "What do you mean?" Gabriella asked.

"Come on," Darren teased Gabriella, oblivious to her discomfort. "You run like—like a wildcat! I mean, you are *fierce* out there. The Willow Cove Clippers were the losingest soccer team in state history until you joined."

"No—" Gabriella began.

"It's true," Darren interrupted her. "Then *you* join the team, and . . . What, you guys have a perfect record now, right? Three and oh?"

Gabriella stared at Darren and Fiona for a

moment—long enough for Fiona to see a glint of gold flash through Gabriella's eyes.

"I thought . . . ," Gabriella moaned, her voice muffled. "Is it really noticeable out there?" She buried her head in her hands.

All of a sudden Darren realized just how upset Gabriella was. "Hey," he said awkwardly. "Don't worry about it. It's not *that* obvious. I mean, I probably only noticed because I know you're a *nahual*, right?"

"Right," Fiona cut in, trying to reassure Gabriella. "How about you, Darren?" she asked, trying to get the unwanted attention off Gabriella. "What did you learn about *impundulus*?"

Darren flipped through his report—it was a lot longer than Fiona's. "You won't believe it," he began. "Making lightning is just the beginning of an *impundulu*'s powers."

Fiona raised an eyebrow. "Yeah?" she asked. "What comes next?"

"*Impundulus* can summon *huge* storms!" Darren continued excitedly. "I bet that's why there was a hurricane surrounding the Changer army during the battle last month. I mean, when you think about it—all those Changers together, in one place . . . We're lucky it wasn't worse."

Fiona shivered. She knew she'd never forget what had happened. A power-hungry warlock, Auden Ironbound, had used an ancient magical horn—the Horn of Power—to bind hundreds of Changers to his will. He swept up the coast with his army under the cover of a hurricane, straight for Willow Cove! Even the First Four, some of the most powerful Changers to ever live, had fallen under Auden Ironbound's spell. Luckily, Fiona, Darren, Mack, and Gabriella were too young to be affected by the horn. Somehow, they'd managed to beat Auden's army, but Auden got away. Everyone knew the warlock would be back.

"Hey, Mack!" Gabriella called.

Mack looked up from his sketch, startled. "Sorry. What did you say?" he asked.

"What are you doing?" Darren asked.

"There's a school-wide art show in a couple weeks," replied Mack. "Everybody in Comics Club is creating a comic to submit."

"Can I see?" asked Gabriella.

Mack shook his head. "Actually, mine is kind of terrible right now," he told her. "Maybe after I figure out a few more panels."

Mack slammed his sketchbook shut, gathered his comics into a pile, and joined the rest of the class.

"So what did you learn about *kitsunes*?" asked Gabriella.

"Well, I learned a lot more about our tails," Mack replied. "Every time a *kitsune* masters a rare power or accomplishes a heroic deed, he or she can earn a new tail, too. A *kitsune* with nine tails is basically the most powerful *kitsune* in the world."

"Dude," Darren said. "Doesn't your *grandfather* have nine tails? In his *kitsune* form, I mean?"

"Exactly," Mack said. "I can't even begin to imagine all the things that Jiichan can do, or the things he accomplished to earn his tails. But get this—when nine-tailed *kitsunes* focus, they can actually see or hear anything in the entire world."

Darren let out a long, low whistle. "No way," he said, clearly impressed.

Mack nodded vigorously. "It's true. They just have to know where to look . . . and it can't be shrouded by magic, of course. That's the catch."

"There's always a catch," Darren groaned. "Still, that's an amazing power."

"Kind of a scary one," Fiona spoke up. "I'm not sure I'd want to be able to do that."

Everyone turned to look at her.

"How about you?" asked Mack. "What did you learn about *selkies*?"

There was a pause before Fiona opened her mouth to reply. Then, just in time, the door opened.

Ms. Therian had arrived.

As she strode across the floor, her long black braid, streaked with silver, swayed behind her. "Your reports, please," she announced, holding out her hand.

Everyone scrambled to pull their reports out of their backpacks. Fiona placed a single piece of paper on top of the stack. Ms. Therian had to notice how much shorter it was than the others, but she didn't say anything.

"And now, for your presentations," Ms. Therian continued. "Let's start with you, Gabriella."

Normally, Fiona would be the first one with her hand in the air—but today, she was all too happy to let someone else go first. She listened attentively to Gabriella's oral report and then Mack's and then Darren's. The facts they had learned about their Changer abilities were so fascinating that Fiona almost forgot the dread she was feeling about her own presentation.

Almost.

"Fiona?" Ms. Therian finally said. "Your turn."

Here goes nothing, Fiona thought as she stood up. She took a few steps forward and then turned to face the bench. Her classmates were smiling at her—not the sarcastic smiles she saw sometimes in her regular classes, but real, true, genuine smiles.

"'The Secrets of *Selkies,*'" Fiona began. "*Selkies* are Changers who take the shape of a seal. They originated in Ireland and Scotland, where tales of *selkies* have been passed down from generation to generation. Every *selkie* is born with a sealskin cloak that allows him or her to transform. Without it, a *selkie* is trapped in his or her human form, so *selkies* must guard their cloaks carefully.

"Like all Changers, *selkies* have powerful abilities,"

Fiona continued. "I wish I could tell you more about them, but I can't. All those human stories about *selkies* are just that—stories—and mostly romances at that. What I can tell you is that *selkie* powers are contained within their songs, which cannot be recorded or captured in any way. The only way to learn a *selkie* song is to be taught by another *selkie*."

Fiona stopped speaking abruptly. There was more she wanted to say about that, but the words seemed stuck in her throat.

"Have you seen another *selkie* before, Fiona?" Ms. Therian asked, filling the silence.

Fiona nodded. "I think so," she said. "During the battle at the beach, I could feel them—in the ocean, I mean. It's like I somehow knew they were nearby."

"Of course," replied Ms. Therian.

"And there's this one *selkie*—I think she's a *selkie*—a beautiful one, with a copper-colored pelt," Fiona continued. "I've seen her twice. From a distance."

"Have you made contact?" Ms. Therian asked evenly.

"No," Fiona said, her voice almost a whisper. "I've been going down to the shore every day for the last three weeks . . . but I haven't seen her since the battle."

Ms. Therian nodded. "I see. You may continue."

Fiona glanced down at her note cards, but she'd already said everything that was written on them. "That's all," she said as her cheeks started to burn with embarrassment.

"Thank you, Fiona," Ms. Therian said.

"I'm sorry," Fiona blurted. "I wanted to do a better job. I spent *hours* researching—"

"You did your best," Ms. Therian cut in. "You know better than any of us how *selkies* are called by the sea. They spend long stretches in the most remote areas of the ocean. Sometimes when they return to land, generations have passed. But I have confidence that you will learn and master all the *selkies'* powers in time."

Fiona returned to the bench and stared straight ahead. Ms. Therian's words had made her feel a little better—and a little curious, too. Who would teach her the *selkie* songs? An image of the copper-colored *selkie* flashed through Fiona's mind. She couldn't wait to see her again . . . but when?

"Now that the presentations are out of the way, I

have some news to share," Ms. Therian continued.

From the tone of her voice, everyone could tell that Ms. Therian's news was big. The mood in the room changed at once.

"The First Four have become aware of a potential new threat from Auden Ironbound," she said. "There is a rare and precious artifact called Circe's Compass. It is no mere navigational tool; rather, it can point the way to any Changer, anywhere in the world. I'm sure you can imagine why Auden Ironbound would desire to possess Circe's Compass—at any cost."

"But Auden Ironbound—wherever he is—has the Horn of Power," Mack spoke up, clearly puzzled. "Once it's repaired, he won't need to know where the Changers are—he can summon and control them. The adults, anyway."

"We're not worried about adult Changers, Mack," Ms. Therian said. "We're worried about you."

Chapter 2
A Family Secret

"Us?" Gabriella asked. She shifted uncomfortably on the hard bench. "But—"

"Auden Ironbound is many things, but stupid is not one of them," Ms. Therian interrupted. "He has likely figured out by now that young Changers are immune to the powers of the horn. He knows you were his undoing. In order to achieve his goals, we believe his next move will be to hunt down young Changers, to remove them from his path. The compass will show him the way to young Changers like you."

It wasn't the words so much as the way Ms. Therian said them that made Gabriella flinch.

"But he doesn't have Circe's Compass yet—does he?" asked Fiona, always practical.

"No," Ms. Therian said slowly. "At least, we don't think so. The truth is that Circe's Compass has been lost for centuries now."

"Lost?" Darren exclaimed. "You mean you don't know where it is?"

"It is locked in a chest that can only be opened by a Changer," Ms. Therian said. "But the location of the chest, I'm afraid, is unknown."

"It doesn't matter if Auden Ironbound finds Circe's Compass," Gabriella said, sounding braver than she felt. "We beat him before. We'll beat him again."

"But wouldn't it be better if *we* find Circe's Compass first?" asked Fiona.

"That's precisely the plan," Ms. Therian explained. "The First Four have already begun investigating. And, as I'm sure you know, magical objects emit their own signals, a beacon of sorts. They're not *that* hard to find— if you know what to look for."

"So . . . you're saying it wouldn't be hard for Auden Ironbound to find it, either?" asked Darren.

There was a strange glint in Ms. Therian's eyes when she answered. "I never said that *he* knows what to look for," she said.

I guess that's supposed to make us feel better, Gabriella thought—but she wasn't very reassured.

"There's a literary festival at New Brighton University on Saturday," Fiona said suddenly. "I could go with my dad and check out the rare books room. It's closed to the public, but my dad has access. We found information on the Horn of Power there. Maybe there will be something about Circe's Compass."

"Want some company?" asked Darren. Like Fiona's dad, Darren's mom was a professor at New Brighton University, and his big brother, Ray, was a student there.

"Sure," replied Fiona. "Anybody else want to come?"

"I wish I could, but I have a game," Gabriella told them.

Mack looked torn. "I was planning to work on my entry for the art show," he said. "But if I finish early, I want to come too."

"Excellent plan," Ms. Therian said. "Remember, I tell you this not to alarm you, but to make you aware. We don't expect Auden Ironbound will be ready to mount another attack for quite some time—but the situation demands constant vigilance all the same. Ultimately, his odds of success increase when we are distracted or fail to pay attention to the signs around us. And on that note, it's time to continue your training. Go ahead and transform so we can get started."

It was like Ms. Therian had said magic words.

Gabriella's transformation to *nahual* was instantaneous—and effortless. It was a tremendous relief to slip into her jaguar self, to see the world through those wide, golden cat's eyes. Hearing about Auden Ironbound and his new plot was unsettling, to say the least. But in her *nahual* form, Gabriella felt ready for anything.

The hint of a smile flickered across Ms. Therian's face as Gabriella stretched her legs, flexing her wide, velvety paws to reveal razor-sharp claws. "Climbing for you today," Ms. Therian said, nodding toward a rocky structure against the far wall of the gym.

Gabriella didn't wait around to hear the others' assignments. The opportunities to be in her *nahual* form were few and far between.

And she wanted to make every moment count.

All too soon, the bell rang. Not only was Changers class over, the school day was, too. For Gabriella, the afternoon was packed: soccer practice; helping her little sister, Maritza, with homework; chores; dinner; starting her own homework. Still, Gabriella lingered in her *nahual* form as she ran one last lap around the gym, a streak of midnight-black fur under the fluorescent lights.

The others clapped when she finished; as Gabriella changed back into her human form, she was already beaming.

"Save some of that for the field, huh?" Mack teased her as he packed his comics.

"Are you kidding?" Gabriella asked as she grabbed her backpack. "I only wish I could."

"It's always best to be discrete—difficult though it may be," Ms. Therian said.

Gabriella turned around quickly. "I was—"

"I know how hard it is," Ms. Therian told her. "Being split between two skins is a challenge few could handle. That's why this space we have—this time we share—is so important. Both of your selves must have the opportunity to be free."

There was a long pause. Ms. Therian opened her mouth, as if there were something more she wanted to say. But all she told them was "See you tomorrow."

Mack and Gabriella watched her leave the Ancillary Gym.

"That was . . . weird," Mack finally said.

"Was it?" Gabriella asked. She couldn't quite tell. Ms. Therian was always very . . . careful about her words.

"I feel like she's trying to tell us something," Mack said. "My grandfather gets like that too. And I'm like, *What*? What are you trying to tell me? Just *say* it; not everything needs to be a riddle or whatever!"

Gabriella started to laugh. "I guess being mysterious is just another thing that the First Four do better than anyone," she joked.

"Wonder when Ms. Therian will teach us about that," Mack said, his eyes gleaming with mischief. He made his voice deeper and said, "The half-truths of a Changer's existence are not truths at all, but lies."

Gabriella applauded. "Perfect! That made, like, zero sense."

"Maybe next time I transform, I'll have earned my

third tail for mysteriousness," Mack joked, making Gabriella laugh again.

She was still smiling in the locker room when she changed into her practice uniform. As she met up with her teammates on the field, Gabriella felt good. Ready. The memory of yesterday's practice was fresh in her mind, but Gabriella wasn't worried. *I got all that* nahual *stuff out of my system in class*, she told herself. *Everything's under control now.*

The whistle blew.

The ball fell.

And Gabriella was off.

She ran so hard that her feet flattened the grass; she ran so fast that her dark ponytail streamed behind her like a blackbird in flight. The sun was bright; it smiled on Gabriella as she dashed down the field. Her kicks were perfectly positioned; perfectly restrained. The ball glided forward as if it were on wings. And it wasn't just Gabriella—the whole team seemed to be playing stronger, tighter, better than ever before, as if every other player was inspired by Gabriella's command of the field.

Like the day before, Gabriella approached Trisha, who was warily blocking the goal. *Better get out of the way, girl,* Gabriella thought as she positioned the ball for one last, solid kick. Gabriella had watched Trisha play goalie plenty of times. She could guess which blocking maneuver Trisha would attempt. But as anticipation rippled through Gabriella's muscles, she knew this was one goal that Trisha could never block.

Gabriella's whole body moved into position for the kick. That solid sense of connection, the leather of her cleat against the leather of the ball . . .

Whooosh!

The ball sailed into the goal. As her teammates erupted into cheers, Gabriella did a fist pump in triumph . . .

And drew blood.

She felt the sharpness slice her palm and glanced at it, perplexed before the pain set in. There was a razor-thin scratch in her skin, not very deep, not very painful, but enough for a line of bright-red blood to seep from it.

How'd I do that? Gabriella wondered.

A closer look told her all she needed to know.

Her fingernails, always clipped short, had transformed into claws. Claws that were two inches long. Claws that ended in sharp, deadly points.

Oh, no, Gabriella thought as a wave of understanding hit her. Panicking was easy. Staying calm—now that was the challenge. She balled up her fists, not even caring if she accidentally sliced her palms again. Then she forced herself to take a deep, slow breath. She'd lost control on the field—there was absolutely zero doubt about that—and somehow, someway, she had to get it back.

I *am in control of my transformations,* Gabriella told herself as she began to count backward from ten. I *am in control of my transformations.*

When she reached zero, Gabriella opened her eyes.

The claws were gone—thankfully.

But had anyone on the team seen them? She glanced warily at the rest of the girls as they helped Trisha pack up the equipment. No one was pointing at Gabriella in shock and horror. No one was even looking at her.

So far, so good, Gabriella thought.

That's when Coach Connors called her name.

Uh-oh, she thought, instantly alert. *Did Coach see my . . . claws? Or . . . my eyes?* Her eyes! Gabriella hadn't even thought about them. If her fingernails had become claws, had her eyes transformed too?

And worse, what if they were still changed?

"I saw what happened on the field," Coach Connors began.

He knows. Gabriella's thoughts raced as she tried to figure out an explanation, an excuse, anything to tell him.

"It's fine to push yourself like that during a practice, but when you're out there on Saturday, pace yourself, okay?" Coach Connors continued. "There are two halves, remember? You don't need to win in the first ten minutes."

"Yeah. Absolutely. I'll remember that," Gabriella heard herself say—boring, ordinary things, not the frantic, fumbling excuses she'd expected to make.

"Great work today, Rivera," Coach Connors told her before turning back to the school building.

And then Gabriella was alone.

She stared at her palm, where the long, red streak was proof that her powers had shown up during practice. Today had been a close call—closer than all the other near misses. Maybe I should talk to Ms. Therian, Gabriella thought. I'm not sure I can handle this by myself.

A pair of arms grabbed Gabriella from behind. She jolted from the surprise, twisted herself away . . .

And looked straight into the familiar brown eyes of her favorite aunt.

"*Mija!*" Tía Rosa exclaimed as she pulled Gabriella toward her and planted a kiss on her forehead.

"Tía Rosa!" shrieked Gabriella as she threw her arms around her aunt's neck. "What are you doing here?"

"My apartment, it's a mess!" Tía Rosa groaned. "All that rain from the hurricane a few weeks ago, it flooded my building, and now we have this disgusting mold problem. The air is so bad. It's very unhealthy."

Gabriella wrinkled her nose. "That's gross!" she replied.

"You said it," Tía Rosa declared. "So the management has to treat the entire building for mold, and all the tenants had to leave for ten days. But that's actually good news for me, because I'm going to be staying with *you!*"

"You are?" Gabriella cried. "For an entire week?" Her *tía* Rosa lived in New Brighton—only an hour away—but her busy work schedule meant that Gabriella didn't get to see her very often.

"That's right," Tía Rosa said, nodding. "I even took time off from work. It's going to be like a vacation with my three favorite girls—you, your sister, and your *mami.*"

"Maybe I should take some time off from school," Gabriella said with a grin.

Tía Rosa chuckled as she linked arms with Gabriella. "Well, you know I would approve, but your mother? Not so much," she said. "Now, let's get home so we can have some fun!"

When Gabriella and Tía Rosa got home a little later, the house seemed empty—at first.

"Ma!" Gabriella called out as she tossed her backpack onto a chair. "Ma? You home?"

"Up here!" Ma's voice was faint, drifting down from the attic.

Gabriella bounded the stairs two at a time, with Tía Rosa right behind her.

Tía Rosa gasped when they reached the attic. "It looks like a bomb went off in here!"

Ma, who was surrounded by boxes and boxes of old papers and photographs, would've been mad if Gabriella had said something like that. But when it came from Rosa, she just laughed. "Found it!" she exclaimed, waving an old scrapbook in the air.

"What's that?" asked Gabriella.

"It's your *abuelita's* old scrapbook from when we were kids," Ma explained. "Tía Rosa said I probably didn't have it anymore. So I set out to prove her wrong."

"I never said that," Tía Rosa protested. "I said you probably couldn't *find* it. Big difference."

"Yeah, the difference being that you were wrong!" Ma teased. "Just you wait, Gabriella, until you see your *tía* with long hair in braids. You won't even recognize her."

Tía Rosa grinned as she ran her fingers through her cropped black hair. "I thought Mami would have a heart attack when I came home from the salon," she said. "I had it all cut off when I was sixteen, and I haven't looked back since!"

Everyone laughed and then Ma's phone started beeping. "Time to pick up Maritza from her piano lesson," she said. "Let's all go together. She'll be so surprised to see you, Rosa! I can't wait to see the look on her face!"

"I like this aunt business," Tía Rosa announced. "Swoop in like a celebrity, get the star treatment. I could get used to this."

"We'll see what you have to say after you help the

girls wash the dishes tonight," Ma teased.

As Gabriella followed her mom and Tía Rosa toward the stairs, she caught her toe on something and tripped in the most spectacular way imaginable. A box skidded across the floor before it hit a rickety old card table, which toppled over—spilling another box of mementos and photos everywhere.

Gabriella tried to stop her fall, but she ended up in a heap on the floor. She groaned as she pulled herself up to a sitting position.

"*Mija!* You okay?" Ma cried as she hurried toward Gabriella.

"Yeah, yeah, I'm just a klutz," Gabriella said, looking down.

"Grab a trash bag, Isabel," Tía Rosa called to Gabriella's mother. "Maybe we can sort through some of this junk while we tidy up."

"No, no, I got it," Gabriella said quickly, looking down at the mess around her. "You go ahead and pick up Maritza," Gabriella continued. "I'll clean up this stuff."

Ma hesitated, but Tía Rosa beamed at Gabriella. "Such a good girl, and so helpful!" she said to her sister.

"Nothing like the two of us when *we* were growing up."

"Yeah . . . but you should see her bedroom," Ma joked.

Then she and Tía Rosa disappeared down the stairs. Their laughter echoed back to Gabriella until they left the house.

Gabriella didn't really mind cleaning up the huge mess she'd made. It was actually pretty interesting—there were photos scattered around that Gabriella had never seen before, of relatives she'd never met. Some of them had been taken in Mexico, where Gabriella's grandmother was born. Gabriella put a few of them in a stack to show Ma and Tía Rosa after dinner. With any luck, they'd start telling one of their stories and forget all about the chores Gabriella and Maritza were supposed to do.

Then something on the floor glinted, catching Gabriella's eye. She wasn't quite sure what it was, but she knew one thing for certain: it definitely wasn't an old photograph.

With careful fingers, Gabriella moved aside the papers that were partially covering the object. Her hands reached for it before she knew what they were doing, as if she was somehow drawn to it.

A *mask*, she thought—but unlike the flimsy, Halloween

store masks she was used to seeing this time of year. This one was tough and aged, made of thick, unyielding leather that had been painted—or dyed?—a shimmery shade of brilliant green. It reminded her of a beetle or a chameleon, reflecting the light with an iridescent gleam.

Looking back, Gabriella was never quite sure why she pulled the mask up to her face and peered through the eye slits. It just seemed, somehow, like the right thing to do. And she certainly never expected the mask to feel so, well, *good*. To Gabriella, who was blinking into the dusty shafts of sunlight filtering through the attic, the mask was suddenly more than a mask. It was a whole new identity. It was a way of concealing what was happening to her. *To hide myself away,* she thought.

The idea was liberating.

And silly, Gabriella realized as she ripped the mask away from her face. Wearing a mask like this in public would probably guarantee *plenty* of attention—and that was the last thing Gabriella wanted.

A yellowed piece of paper fluttered to the floor. Gabriella picked it up and realized that it was a newspaper clipping.

ROBBERY THWARTED!
Emerald Wildcat Saves the Day

An attempted robbery of New Brighton Central Bank was thwarted on Thursday by a masked individual who, witnesses claimed, apprehended the suspects and tied them to the bank's marble columns. Witnesses reported that the hero then transformed into a leopard or jaguar before fleeing the scene, shortly before police arrived.

"It's very common for mass hysteria, or even psychosis, to occur in groups of people who are under extreme stress or facing life-threatening danger," said Dr. Abigail Lansing, chair of New Brighton University's psychology department.

Gabriella carefully placed the article on the floor. She didn't need to read any more about Dr. Lansing's opinions. Most people might find it hard—impossible, even—to believe that the witnesses were right.

But not Gabriella.

It had *to be a* nahual, she thought as she turned the mask over in her hands. *Right in New Brighton—just an hour away!*

Gabriella reached for the article again and stared at the blurry photo beneath the headline. Taken from the bank's security-camera footage, it wasn't great quality, but if Gabriella squinted, she could get a better look at the hero who had single-handedly stopped the robbery. She had long glossy black hair, which was slicked back from her face. *Her face!* Gabriella thought. If only she could see the face behind the mask—

But her neck was visible, and so was her chin. It was a silly thought—just thinking it made Gabriella blush, even though she was all alone in the attic—but for a moment, Gabriella thought she recognized herself in those features.

Don't be ridiculous, Gabriella scolded herself.

And yet . . .

The mask felt so right. Normal, even, for someone who thought she'd left that word behind the first time she transformed.

Why is this even here? Gabriella wondered suddenly. In an attic filled with old photos and family heirlooms, the mask and newspaper clipping were completely out of place.

Or were they?

A new idea struck Gabriella then, as sudden and unexpected as one of the lightning bolts that crackled between Darren's fingers.

Changer ability runs in families, she thought, sitting up straighter. *Ms. Therian said so. Just look at Mack and his grandfather!*

Gabriella hardly dared to think it, but she couldn't stop herself.

Could I be related to the Emerald Wildcat? she mused.

Then she heard the sound of a door opening.

"Gabriella! We're home!" Ma called from downstairs.

"Be right there!" Gabriella called back, trying to make her voice sound as normal as possible as she shoved the mask into her hoodie's pocket. One afternoon in the attic, and her whole world had shifted. Because if Ma was a *nahual* too, if everything that was happening to Gabriella had happened to Ma and she'd somehow survived it and become so good at concealing her true self that even her own daughters didn't know . . .

Then maybe there was hope for Gabriella after all.

Chapter 3
Under Control

Mack got to school so early the next morning that the cafeteria was still serving breakfast. Even though he could smell French toast sticks and maple syrup, he went straight to homeroom. He had so much work to do on his comic that every second of the day counted—and Mack would rather steal fifteen extra minutes to sketch in homeroom than have a second breakfast in the cafeteria.

Using the side of his pencil, Mack made some thick broad lines on his paper. The kind of comic art he loved had dark, heavy lines, which were perfect for conveying energy and action. Detail work, Mack had already

discovered, was harder. Facial features, for example—
How did anybody ever learn to draw two eyes of the same
shape, or a mouth that was more than a cartoony loop?

Practice, probably, Mack thought, grimacing as he
erased his superhero's face again. The paper wouldn't
hold up to much more erasing, but Mack didn't mind if
he had to start over. He would do whatever it took to get
the facial expression *just* right.

Mack was so engrossed in his sketching that he
didn't even hear when someone had come up behind
him, whispering "*Psst!*" to get his attention. It wasn't
until a hand grabbed his right shoulder—jostling his
drawing hand—that he looked up.

"Hey! What—" he started to say. But when Mack realized that Gabriella was standing next to him, he softened.

"Hey, Gabriella. What's up?" he asked. A confused
expression flickered across his face. "This isn't your
homeroom. Is something wrong?"

"No . . . not wrong, exactly," Gabriella began. She
glanced over her shoulder at the door to make sure no
one was about to join them.

"What's going on?" Mack said.

Gabriella didn't reply as she slipped the Emerald Wildcat's mask out of her backpack. Mack let out a low whistle. He turned it over and over in his hands, examining the iridescent leather, before he looked up at Gabriella.

"Pretty awesome mask," he said as he handed it back to her. "Where did you get it?"

"In my attic, actually," Gabriella explained. "I think . . . I know this sounds crazy, Mack, but I think it belonged to a real superhero. A *Changer* superhero—a *nahual* one, to be specific."

Mack's eyes widened, flashing with excitement and intrigue. "Are you kidding?" he asked. But before Gabriella could tell him more, Mack started rummaging through his backpack. "Check this out," he said as he held out a comic book.

It was old; Gabriella could tell that right away. The paper felt thin and worn, as though someone had flipped through it hundreds of times. The date on the cover read May 20, 1996. But Gabriella couldn't tear her eyes away from the title. In tall, jagged letters, it read *The Emerald Wildcat, Volume 1.*

Gabriella couldn't speak.

There she was, on the cover—or at least, a drawing of her: The Emerald Wildcat, a gorgeous Latina, wearing a green leather suit. Her black hair shone with blue highlights, and her eyes—striking, unmistakable golden cat's eyes—stared through a shimmering green mask.

The same mask that Gabriella held in her hands.

"I—I don't understand," she finally said.

"The Emerald Wildcat. A lesser-known superhero, but one of the coolest, in my humble opinion. One of the most amazing things about the Emerald Wildcat is that she really existed. For a few years in, uh, the mid-nineties, she actually stopped a bunch of crimes from happening—right in New Brighton," Mack said, sounding a little bit like a superhero encyclopedia. "Here, I think there's an article online...."

Mack tapped his phone a few times and then showed the screen to Gabriella. "All the archives of the *New Brighton Times* are online now," he told her. "Pretty cool, huh?"

"I found a copy of that article in my attic!" Gabriella exclaimed. She would've recognized the grainy photo anywhere.

"Right, so the Emerald Wildcat was running around town, fighting all this crime—better than the police, even," Mack continued. "And *everybody* wanted to find out who she was! But she left, like, no clues. Ever. Then things . . . changed."

"What do you mean?" asked Gabriella.

"Like, the police put out a wanted poster with her mask on it," Mack explained, flipping to a panel near the back of the comic. "They were so embarrassed. Here was this so-called superhero—I mean, nobody believed she was an actual wildcat, because . . . well, you know. And she was doing a better job at stopping crime than the actual police!"

"So what happened to her?" Gabriella said.

Mack shrugged. "Nobody knows. She simply . . . disappeared, never to be heard from again. Of course, her adventures live on in the Emerald Wildcat comic series. They retold some of her exploits and invented new ones after she vanished. But as for the Emerald Wildcat herself . . . It's almost like she never existed."

"But she *did* exist!" Gabriella said, forgetting to whisper as she waved the mask in the air. "And—and—I think she's my *mom!*"

"No *way!*" Mack exclaimed loudly. Then he glanced anxiously over his shoulder. "I mean . . ."

"Think about it," Gabriella urged. "It makes sense, right? The Emerald Wildcat was obviously a *nahual* Changer. And Changer abilities run in families. A*nd* her mask was in my attic! I mean, that can't be a coincidence!

"Plus, my mom grew up in New Brighton," Gabriella continued. "She only moved to Willow Cove after I was born."

"I can't believe it," Mack said, his voice full of admiration. "I'm actually friends with the daughter of a *superhero!* This is without a doubt *the* most incredible—"

"Good morning, Mr. Kimura," Mr. Morrison, Mack's homeroom teacher, said as he walked into the classroom. "You're here early."

Gabriella shoved the Emerald Wildcat's mask into her hoodie's pocket; the sudden motion made Mr. Morrison glance in her direction. She wasn't doing anything wrong, but she still felt guilty from the way he raised an eyebrow as he looked at her. "I suppose you'd better be off to your own homeroom, Ms. Rivera," he said. "The first bell is about to ring."

"Yes, Mr. Morrison," Gabriella said. Then, under her breath, she whispered to Mack, "Talk to you later."

"Here," Mack said suddenly as he pressed *The Emerald Wildcat, Volume I* into her hands. "You can borrow it."

For just a moment, Gabriella hesitated.

Why would she want some dumb comic? Mack asked himself, feeling a little embarrassed. *She probably thinks they are the ultimate in uncool.*

But to Mack's surprise, Gabriella grinned at him. "Thanks," she replied gratefully. "I can't *wait* to read it."

Later that day, Mack ran all the way to the Ancillary Gym for Changers class. His plan to sneak in a few extra minutes of drawing time during lunch had worked a little *too* well. Hunkered in the stairwell, he hadn't heard the bell signaling the end of lunch—or even realized it had rung until a bunch of kids were stepping around him on their way to the upstairs classrooms. By the time Mack reached the Ancillary Gym, everyone else had already transformed and started practicing. One look at the steely expression in Ms. Therian's eyes told him that he was in trouble.

"I'm . . . sorry," Mack panted. "It won't . . . happen . . . again."

Ms. Therian nodded—just once. "Go ahead and transform, Mack," she told him. "You and Gabriella will be racing today."

Mack transformed and then glanced over to the track, where Gabriella was waiting for him in her *nahual* form. Since Mack and Gabriella were the two land-based Changers, it made sense for them to be paired up. That didn't bother Mack one bit. The same skills that made Gabriella such a formidable force on the soccer field challenged Mack in his training, pushing him to be faster . . . stronger . . . better. He hadn't won a race against Gabriella yet, but he was determined to keep trying.

Gabriella's long, sleek tail flicked back and forth, like a wave, as Mack joined her on the track. Her eyes, shining and golden, seemed like they were smiling at him.

Ready to race? Gabriella's voice echoed in his head.

Oh, it's on, he said back to her.

At the first shriek of a whistle, Mack was off and running.

Sometimes Mack wondered if his heightened

kitsune senses were the reason why he could never quite catch Gabriella. The feel of his paws propelling him forward, the light glinting off the equipment in the gym, and the sounds echoing off the walls were a constant distraction. If there was a way to turn down his senses, Mack hadn't figured it out yet.

Boom! There was Gabriella, her large paws thundering on the indoor track's spongy surface.

Splash! There was Fiona in her *selkie* form, struggling to master her swimming ability by diving through a series of increasingly narrow hoops.

Flash! There was Darren, *impundulu* wings outstretched as he perched high on an exposed pipe near the ceiling. Small sparks crackled from the end of his talons. With Mack's keen fox vision, he could see the determined gleam in Darren's eyes. *You can do it,* Mack thought to him.

In that same instant the bolt of lightning ripped through the room. Was it coincidence? Or had Mack accidentally distracted Darren?

It all happened so fast—that burning bolt of electricity that sliced through the air. Mack watched, horrified, as it missed the pool where Fiona swam, blissfully unaware, by inches.

Thweeeeeet!

The call from Ms. Therian's whistle captured everyone's attention.

"Human forms, please," she said, her voice trembling.

If Darren's lightning bolt had hit the pool while Fiona was swimming . . ., Mack thought as he transformed. He shook his head. It was too terrible to think about—all that water, electrified, and Fiona trapped in the middle of it . . .

"Did you see that?" Gabriella, who was back in her human form, asked him.

Mack nodded. "Close call, huh?"

"Too close, I bet," she replied in a low voice. "Ms. Therian looked like she was going to have a heart attack."

Mack tilted his head. Ms. Therian's face *did* look pretty gray.

"That was a good practice," Ms. Therian announced as everyone gathered around her. "Mack, very nice form while sprinting. You seem more comfortable as a *kitsune* every time you transform."

Then Ms. Therian turned to Darren. "Darren—"

"I'm sorry," he said right away. "I didn't *mean* to send out any lightning—"

"It happens," she interrupted him. "After all, practice is the purpose of this class. Still, I think it would be wise to take additional precautions. Whenever Fiona is in the pool, you should practice on the opposite side of the gym."

"Of course," Darren replied. Then he turned to Fiona. "Sorry about that."

She smiled at him. "No harm, no foul," she said.

"Fiona, you need to continue practicing your breathing exercises," Ms. Therian continued.

"In the ocean?" Fiona asked hopefully.

But Ms. Therian shook her head. "I would prefer you work on them in a controlled environment. However, I suppose you could practice in your bathtub at home."

For some reason the thought of Fiona as a seal, lounging in a bath tub, was hilariously funny. Even Fiona laughed, though her cheeks burned bright red at the same time. And just like that, the anxious tension that had filled the room from Darren's stray lightning bolt melted away.

"And Gabriella . . . ," Ms. Therian began.

Mack's head turned, just a little. Whatever advice Gabriella was about to receive, he wanted to hear it, too.

But Ms. Therian didn't comment on Gabriella's performance during practice. Instead, Ms. Therian tapped her own temple and said simply, "Mind your eyes."

All the kids looked at Gabriella just in time to see her golden cat's eyes shimmer and shift to brown human eyes. "Thanks," she said. "I need all the reminders I can get."

Gabriella seemed ready to say more, but closed her mouth instead. She pulled a small compact out of her backpack and glanced at her eyes to double-check.

"Enjoy your weekend," Ms. Therian said as she dismissed them. Then she crossed the room to examine the spot where Darren's lightning bolt had struck the floor.

Everyone hung out by the bench while they waited for the final bell.

"So my dad says we need to leave by eight thirty tomorrow morning," Fiona said to Darren. "Pick you up at eight twenty?"

Darren grimaced. "I usually have a strict policy

against setting my alarm clock on a Saturday," he said. "But for beating Auden Ironbound, I'm willing to make an exception."

"I really wish I could come with you guys," Gabriella said wistfully.

"Don't worry about it," Fiona told her. "It's better that you show up for the soccer game like normal."

"Yeah," Mack agreed. He shifted uncomfortably. "Do you guys, uh, need me to come? My project is still really far behind. . . ."

"I think we've got it under control," Fiona said. "Darren and I were a pretty good team when we researched in the rare books room before."

"Yeah, you should stay home and keep working on your comic," Darren told Mack. "Practice makes perfect, after all. And speaking of practice . . ."

Everyone turned to look as he held up his right hand and snapped his fingers. A shower of sparks flew into the air, like a burning log shifting in a campfire. The sparks hovered for a moment and then twinkled as they fell and faded.

"Do it again!" Fiona cried.

With a confident grin, Darren snapped his fingers several times. The shower flew fast, making a golden cloud. There was a strange expression on Gabriella's face as she reached out to touch it.

"Don't—" Fiona began.

But it was too late. They heard a sizzle, and then Gabriella sucked in her breath sharply and popped her index finger into her mouth.

"Oh man," Darren said anxiously. "Did you get burned? I am *so* sorry, Gabriella. I would never—"

"Not your fault," Gabriella said, managing a smile. "I should know better than to play with fire."

"Cat's eyes," Mack said suddenly, louder than he intended.

"What?" Gabriella asked, and something like panic flashed in her face. "I don't—I just looked in the mirror and they were *fine*."

"Maybe the sparks?" Fiona suggested. "I have this theory that Changer powers can feed off one another—"

The final bell rang then, and as everyone grabbed their backpacks, Mack glanced at Gabriella's eyes. "They're still gold," he whispered. "Maybe you should—"

"Gabriella," Ms. Therian interrupted him. "Would you stay after class, please?"

Gabriella nodded, looking miserable. She didn't say a word.

Way to go, Mack thought angrily. *You just got her in trouble. Why can't you learn to keep your mouth shut?*

Though Fiona and Darren headed toward the doors, Mack leaned down, pretending to tie his shoe. If Gabriella was going to be yelled at, he wanted to be there to stick up for her.

"Gabriella," Ms. Therian began.

"I know. I'm sorry. I don't know why this keeps happening," Gabriella spoke up, the words tumbling out in a rush. "Really, I'm trying my hardest to make sure—"

"You don't need to apologize," Ms. Therian told her, somehow sounding stern and sympathetic at the same time. "*Never* apologize for who you truly are."

A long silence followed.

"But you do need to be careful," Ms. Therian finally continued. "If you go out into the world before your transformation is complete, everyone could learn your secret. *Our* secret. I'd recommend cooling down more before practice ends. . . ."

Mack couldn't imagine what it would be like to transform when he least expected it. To have something so important be completely out of his control. He glanced at Gabriella out of the corner of his eye and tried to catch her attention. He wanted to smile, to wave, to do *something* to make her feel better.

But Gabriella was staring at the floor . . . and she wouldn't look up for anything.

Chapter 4
THE RARE BOOKS ROOM

Despite his grumbling about the early start, Darren was ready and waiting for Fiona and her dad when they arrived to pick him up on Saturday. Darren's best friends, Ethan and Kyle, were always complaining about how late he was. It was a habit he was trying to break. Fiona's dad honked the horn in greeting as Darren bounded down the front steps two at a time and climbed into the backseat.

"Breakfast?" Fiona asked as she held out a box of doughnuts.

"Definitely!" Darren replied as he grabbed a chocolate one with sprinkles on top. "Thanks! And thanks for the ride, Mr. Murphy. Or do you prefer Professor Murphy?"

"You can call me Mr. Murphy," Fiona's dad said with a chuckle. "Only my students have to call me 'professor.' And I'm happy to give you two a ride to campus. I'm very impressed by you both—spending a beautiful Saturday in the library, working on your book reports. I can't say I was that responsible when I was your age."

Darren glanced into the side mirror and caught Fiona's eye. From the way she raised her eyebrow, he could tell that she wanted him to play along.

"Well, you know. Gotta get it done," Darren said. "My mom always says— I think you know my mom, Sharon Smith? She's a professor in the chemistry department?"

"Yes, Fiona mentioned that," Mr. Murphy said. "A very impressive scholar. I don't know her very well, but I heard she won a pretty prestigious research grant last month. . . ."

For the entire hour-long drive to New Brighton University, Darren kept up a steady stream of chatter with Fiona and her dad. When they arrived on campus, Mr. Murphy rummaged through his wallet and pulled out a plastic card. "This is my faculty key card," he explained. "Remember, the rare books room is technically closed on weekends, but you should be able to access everything you need through the digitized versions on the computers. If there's any problem with that, just use my key card to get into the rare books room, where you can find all the original source materials."

"Thanks, Dad," Fiona replied as she slipped it into her pocket. "Meet you for lunch?"

"Sounds like a plan," Mr. Murphy said. "I'll see you in the dining hall at noon. Good luck with your reports!"

As soon as he was out of earshot, Fiona turned to Darren. "Sorry," she said in a low voice. "I had to make up an excuse for why we needed to be in the library. Thanks for playing along."

"No worries," Darren told her. "I don't think he suspected anything."

"You're really good at that," Fiona said.

Darren's face wrinkled in confusion. "Good at what?" he asked.

"I don't know, *talking* to people," she said. "It seems so easy for you. Like you always know what to say. I can never think of the right thing to say until, like, five minutes too late."

Darren was surprised. Supersmart Fiona had trouble coming up with the right thing to say? That was news to him. "That's not how you come across," Darren reassured her.

"Really?" she asked.

Darren shrugged. "To me it's like . . . like you're only going to speak up if you have something worth saying," he said. "That's why when you talk, people listen."

Fiona blinked rapidly as she glanced away, but Darren thought he saw the hint of a smile on her face. "We should get to the rare books room," she said. "I hope we can find what we need quickly, but if not . . ."

Darren had only been in the rare books room once before, when he and Fiona had accidentally run into each other while their parents were at work. After they had decided to start research for their Changers reports, Fiona had introduced him to the rare books room, her favorite place on campus. What they'd learned there about Auden Ironbound's Horn of Power had helped them prepare for the battle of their lives.

Would they be so lucky a second time?

Fiona seemed to think so. *Is she humming?* Darren wondered as they walked through the library to the rare books room and the computer bank outside it. Every so often, he swore he could faintly hear a few pretty, high-pitched notes. *Bet that's her* selkie *side,* Darren thought, smiling to himself. He would've cracked a joke, but Fiona seemed so happy, he didn't want to spoil it.

Maybe the rare books room really is her favorite place, he mused.

This corner of the library was practically deserted, except for three college guys who were hunched over a computer at the far end of the room.

"This isn't right," one of them was saying. He tugged at the collar on his shirt and then ran his hand across his damp forehead. "It should be here! If—"

"Jack, would you *shut up*?" the one sitting at the keyboard hissed. "I'm trying to find it, okay?"

"Why don't *you* shut up, Bram?" Jack shot back. "If this is you trying, I'd hate to see you fail."

"Enough," the third guy, the one in the red New Brighton University hat, said. There was something in his voice that silenced both his friends.

Man, college must be really rough, Darren thought. He couldn't imagine ever talking to his friends like that—especially not over some school project. "Let's use this one," he murmured to Fiona, gesturing to a computer a few feet away from the guys.

Fiona immediately sat down at the keyboard and entered her dad's log-in info. "I can't wait to go here," she confided in Darren. "Have my own ID, my own key card—everything."

"Yeah, I guess," he said. "I haven't thought about it much. But my brother seems pretty happy."

Fiona typed quickly—far quicker than Darren could. "This one," she said as the cursor of the mouse hovered over a title: *Traditions of Otherworldly Beings.* "I'm sure that's the one we looked at before."

"So the whole thing's been scanned?" Darren asked.

Fiona nodded. "It's to protect the rare books," she explained. "Anytime they're touched by human hands, they can be damaged. The good news is that since the book has been digitized, we can use the search function now."

Fiona's fingers clicked on the keyboard as she typed the phrase "Circe's Compass" into the search box.

Darren and Fiona waited a few seconds. Then a message flashed across the screen: NO RESULTS FOUND.

"Uh-oh," Darren said.

But Fiona shook her head. "Not a problem, I just don't have the right term yet," she said. "Sometimes words were spelled differently a long time ago."

Darren watched as Fiona typed in "Circe" and then "Cyrce" and then "Kirke," and several other variations. Finally, she tried simply "compass."

But the same message—NO RESULTS FOUND— appeared for every term she searched.

A puzzled frown crossed Fiona's face. "I find it very hard to believe that a book with more than a thousand pages from this era doesn't have a single reference to a compass," she said.

"Maybe the spelling's not quite right," Darren suggested. "Or it had a completely different name back then."

"Maybe," Fiona replied, but her voice was doubtful. "Still, there should be . . . something . . ."

Suddenly, Fiona sat up straighter. As her fingers flew across the keys, Darren realized that she'd had an idea.

That's also when he realized that the guys across the room had gotten very quiet.

And they were watching them.

Darren turned back to the computer just in time to see that same, frustrating message flashing again.

NO RESULTS FOUND

"I was right!" Fiona cried. "See, I searched for 'Horne of Power'—weird spelling and all—because we know for a *fact* that it has a listing in this book, right, and I remember *exactly* how it's spelled, and get this! The computer *still* says no results were found!"

"Shhh," Darren said with a nervous glance to the guys. To his relief, though, they were engrossed in their own computer again. "So . . . what exactly does that mean?"

"I can't say for certain," Fiona replied. "There might be a problem with the search function. I don't know. But I *do* know what we can do about it."

"What?" asked Darren.

Fiona stood up abruptly. "Examine the source!"

With her dad's key card in hand, Fiona strode toward

the locked room that held all the ancient, irreplaceable volumes. The moment she swiped the card, Darren could hear the whir of the lock opening.

"Come on," Fiona said, pushing open the door. She pulled out a drawer that was near the entrance and withdrew two pairs of pristine white cotton gloves. "Safety first . . . Well, the books' safety, that is."

Darren laughed as he pulled on the silly gloves.

In seconds, Fiona was halfway across the rare books room, reaching for *Traditions of Otherworldly Beings*. With extreme care, Fiona gingerly laid the book on the table and flipped it open to page 258. Her eyes darted back and forth as she scanned the page.

Then she shook her head.

"It's . . . Something . . . Something's wrong," she said. "I *know* this is the right book, but there's no mention of the Horn of Power—and there should be."

"Maybe it was on another page," Darren offered.

Fiona shook her head again. "I distinctly remember the page number," she insisted. "I'm sure of it."

Darren was about to ask if Fiona had a photographic memory when she suddenly sucked in her breath sharply.

"What? What is it?" Darren asked, immediately on edge.

"Look," Fiona breathed. "Look at the words!"

If Darren hadn't seen it with his own eyes, he never would have believed it: The letters shivered, trembled, and then began to shift and swirl across the page like a swarm of snakes. His mouth fell open from shock.

"It—did—" Darren stammered, at a loss for words. "Why didn't it do this before? The last time we looked at it?"

"I don't know—it must be a magical defense mechanism!" Fiona glanced up at him, her face shining with joy. "It's the right page," she whispered. Her gloved finger hovered above the heading, which now clearly read "HORNE OF POWER." "It's the right text!"

"How?" Darren asked in amazement.

"Some sort of enchantment, I assume," Fiona said, a note of awe in her voice. "There's information here that is so sacred—so powerful—that only certain eyes can see it. And the book somehow *knows*—"

"Check the index!" Darren exclaimed. "Look for Circe's Compass!"

He eagerly reached for the book, but Fiona stopped him. "It's so fragile," she said. "We still need to be careful."

"Hey," a new voice said.

Darren and Fiona looked up to see the three guys from the computer station.

They were blocking the door.

Almost by instinct, Fiona closed the book and held it against her chest, as if she could protect it.

"Can we take a look?" the guy in the red hat said. His smile was bright, but his eyes . . . There was something wrong with them, a flat emptiness that gave Darren a sudden chill.

We have to get out of here.

Just as Darren thought those words, they seemed to echo in his head—but in Fiona's voice, the same way they communicated in their Changer forms.

So she felt it too—magic.

"A quick look," the guy continued, still pretending to be friendly. He took a step forward. His friends moved forward too. But the solid bookshelf against Darren's back told him there was nowhere to run.

"Give me the book," the guy in the red hat continued. His smile faded until his face was as malevolent as his eyes.

"Just grab it, Evan!" Bram snapped, agitated.

Fiona shoved the massive book into her backpack, just as Evan's fist erupted with glowing magic.

What choice did Darren have?

The thunderbolt was forming at his fingertips before he had figured out a plan, but the moment he felt that fiery crackling—the very second it started—Darren realized what he had to do.

It was blisteringly hot. . . .

And blindingly bright . . .

But he flung it at them, anyway.

"Come on!" Darren shouted over their howls as he grabbed Fiona's hand.

Darren and Fiona ran—leaping over the three guys and darting through the doorway. Were those guys wounded—or worse? Darren swallowed hard. He couldn't bear to find out.

"Where are we going?" Fiona gasped as Darren dragged her down the stairs.

"Somewhere safe," he replied shortly, pushing himself to run faster. If only he could transform, could fly away on his strong *impundulu* wings and take Fiona with him . . .

"Darren!" she exclaimed. "They're following us!"

"No," he said. "That's not possible. I *saw* the lightning hit them. . . ."

But one glance over his shoulder confirmed Fiona's claim.

And perhaps even harder to believe, there wasn't a single sign they'd been hit by lightning. No scars, no singed clothes. The guys looked perfectly normal as they scanned the crowd.

They're looking for us, Darren thought, panicked, as a feeling of dread settled in the pit of his stomach.

Darren pulled Fiona into a crowd of students who were listening to a drum circle in the quad. They wove through the crowd while Darren frantically tried to come up with a plan. *Even if we lose them out here*, he thought, *we're still exposed. And they likely know this campus better than we do.*

There was only one thing to do: hide.

Fortunately, Darren knew just where to go.

There were plenty of buildings on campus that Darren had never visited before, but his big brother's dorm was unmistakable. It was a sleek, shiny building covered in glass panels; the newest dorm stood out from all the other ivy-covered brick halls—which meant Darren could find it in an instant.

Darren and Fiona never stopped running as Darren dug around in his pocket, found his cell phone, and desperately dialed Ray's number. *Please answer,* Darren thought anxiously as he and Fiona reached the locked dorm. *Please, Ray. Answer your phone!*

Darren glanced anxiously over his shoulder. There, not far away, a flash of red—a baseball cap . . .

They've found us, he thought.

"Hey, bro! What's up?"

The sound of Ray's voice almost made Darren cry with relief.

"Ray! I'm downstairs!" Darren babbled into his phone. "Can you—can you—the door—"

"Sure, let me buzz you in," Ray said.

Bzzzzzzzzzzzzzzzz.

Darren yanked on the door so hard that it shuddered. "Hurry!" he yelled as he and Fiona dashed into the building.

The door shut behind them with a reassuring click.

That, Darren knew, was the automatic lock resetting—but he wouldn't feel at ease until they were safe in Ray's dorm room.

"This way," he told Fiona as he led her up a flight of stairs, which seemed safer than waiting around in the glass-paneled lobby for the elevator. Luckily, Ray's room was on the third floor. He was waiting for them in the doorway when they arrived. But one look at their faces made his smile fade.

"Darren, what's wrong?" Ray asked.

"I . . . ," Darren began, panting. He bent over with his hands on his knees as he tried to catch his breath.

"Hi, I'm Ray," Ray introduced himself to Fiona. His forehead was creased with worry. "Are you two okay?"

Fiona swallowed hard. "Yeah. We were working on our book reports and we—we kind of got lost," she said, thinking fast. "But Darren recognized your dorm, so, uh, it's all good now. I'm Fiona, by the way."

Ray's face relaxed. "Oh, good. You had me worried for a minute," he replied. "Are you seriously winded from the stairs?"

"Yeah," Darren said, laughing nervously. "Sorry—I

was completely turned around. I couldn't even find the cafeteria."

Ray laughed loudly. "Now *that's* hard to believe," he joked. "I have to go meet my study group. Want me to show you where to get some lunch?"

Fiona and Darren exchanged a glance. On the one hand, they'd probably be safer with Ray to escort them around campus . . . but then again, what could Ray do to protect them against three warlocks?

"Actually, can we hang out here for a while?" Darren asked.

"You don't even have to ask," Ray said, flashing a smile. "Text me if you need anything. I'll be down at the library."

Darren forced himself to return Ray's smile as he remembered the terror he'd felt, being chased by the warlocks among the stacks of books. "Thanks, bro. I'll see you soon."

"Family dinner next weekend," Ray reminded him. "You make sure Dad's there; I'll make Mom drive me home. Nice to meet you, Fiona. You two stay out of trouble now."

Then Ray grabbed his backpack and left. Neither Darren nor Fiona spoke until the door had closed behind him.

"Easier said than done," Fiona blurted out.

Darren looked at her, confused. "What?" he asked.

"Staying out of trouble," she explained. "It's easier said than done. Those guys . . . They were—"

"Magic," Darren finished for her.

Fiona reached into her backpack for the book, which was nestled in the soft folds of her *selkie* cloak. Then she paused. "Does Ray have a roommate?" she asked.

Darren shook his head. "This is a single room," he said. "It's safe."

With extreme caution, Fiona brought the ancient book out of her backpack. Then she laughed suddenly, making Darren jump.

"What is it?" he asked.

Fiona held up her gloved hands. "I just realized I'm still wearing these!"

Darren watched over Fiona's shoulder as she placed the book on Ray's desk. When she opened it, her hand hovered over the words—and once again, they rearranged themselves, moving around the page like fallen leaves scattered by a gust of wind. When they settled again, the text was clear:

Circe's Compasse

Useful in the Search for Changers, Circe's Compasse was closely held by the Bonekamp Family until the Time of the Dark, when it was Lost amid the carnage. Some 400 years later, it Resurfaced during the reign of Ilyana the Conqueror. In Recognition of the extreme Power and Usefulness of Circe's Compasse, it was secreted away in the Year 1792, secured in a Magic Chest on the Seafarer, a ship bound for the Americas. Alas, a storm claimed the ship, its crew, and cargo near the coast of the settlement at Middletown.

Fiona's white-gloved finger trembled as she pointed to the word "Middletown." "Darren!" she breathed. "Middletown is *right next* to Willow Cove!"

"I don't know," he replied, still staring at the text.

"There are lots of Middletowns. There's a chance it might not be the one near us."

As if on cue the book produced a map of the coast. There was Middletown, and not far from it, Willow Cove.

"See? It *is* the same one. Circe's Compass is *close!*" Fiona cried in excitement. "And if the ship wasn't salvaged—if no Changer ever found it—then Circe's Compass may be at the bottom of the ocean!"

Darren was still staring at the book. "'The Time of the Dark,'" he said suddenly. "What—what do you think that means?"

Fiona shivered. "I have no idea," she admitted. "We could ask Ms. Therian, I guess."

"Or we could ask the book," Darren pointed out.

Fiona hesitated, but only for a moment. Then she purposefully turned the page and waited for the letters to shift.

But they didn't move.

As fast as she dared, Fiona flipped through the pages, scanning each one for "Time of the Dark." But the phrase never appeared again.

"This book," she marveled. "I've never seen anything like it. It shows you what you need to know. I feel like—like it's *writing* itself."

Darren rubbed his neck, trying to get rid of the creepy, prickly feeling that was spreading across his skin. "I don't like it," he said. "It's weird."

"It's *wonderful*," Fiona corrected him, wrapping the book in her *selkie* cloak and safely stashing it into her backpack. "Come on. Let's go find my dad. We've got to go home—there isn't any time to waste!"

Home, to Willow Cove; home, near Middletown; home, to the coast where that sunken ship and all its mysteries rested at the bottom of the sea. Darren knew it was the right thing to do—the smart thing, even. It certainly wasn't safe for them to stick around here much longer, not when those guys were probably still searching for them.

Chapter 5
THE BIG GAME

Back in Willow Cove, Gabriella stood by the side of the soccer field and chugged a bottle of water. It was hard to believe the game was already half over; for Gabriella, it had passed by in a blur as she raced up and down the field. Her muscles were twitching with eagerness to get back out there and win this game. The Willow Cove Clippers had never played better, but for Gabriella, that wasn't good enough. She wanted them to be the best in state. The best *ever*.

"*Mija!*" Tía Rosa said, beaming as she approached. "You run like the wind out there!"

"Tía Rosa!" Gabriella exclaimed. "Thanks—but you

shouldn't be down here. Fans have to stay in the bleachers. If Coach saw you . . ."

Tía Rosa waved her hand in the air. "Pssh, what do I care?" she said. "If anybody has a problem with me telling my niece what an amazing athlete she is, they can say it to my face."

"You've gotta get out of here." Gabriella laughed as she gave Tía Rosa a kiss on the cheek and then nudged her back to the stands. "I'll find you after the game."

"Find me? You won't be able to miss me," Tía Rosa teased. "I'll be the one down front, screaming your name!"

Thweeeet!

When the ref blew his whistle, Tía Rosa scurried back to the bleachers, and Gabriella prepared to take the field again. The unexpected halftime visit from her aunt had supercharged Gabriella. Now she felt like *anything* was possible out on the field—but most of all, she wanted to make her aunt proud.

This half is for Tía Rosa, Gabriella thought suddenly. *To show her what I can really do.*

That thought, more than any other, pushed Gabriella

to do her best. She scored goal after goal, dodging every opposing player who tried to block her. There were no other thoughts on Gabriella's mind but how free she felt, how powerful. She no longer felt like she was running on the field, but dancing, flying. For Gabriella, it wasn't a game anymore.

It was everything.

And then it all went wrong.

A sudden pop, like a balloon bursting at a little kid's birthday party; a swift hiss of air. There was no smooth, seamless arc for the ball; no sail across the clear blue sky. Instead, the ball fell to the ground with a dull thud.

No one moved.

It took a few seconds for Gabriella to realize exactly what had happened: Somehow, the ball had burst. *But how?* she wondered numbly.

The referee jogged across the field, blowing his whistle. The rest of the players crowded around him as he knelt down to inspect the ball. Even from a distance, Gabriella could see the problem clearly: a gaping, four-inch gash across the soccer ball's scuffed surface.

How did that happen? Gabriella mused. As she stepped

forward to take a better look, her foot caught in the grass and she nearly tripped. Steadying herself just in time, Gabriella glanced down—and saw a row of sharp claws sticking out of her shoe.

No, Gabriella thought, her heart pounding with panic. No!

She'd felt so confident on the field, so in control. But now here she was, her own *nahual* claws jutting out of her cleats for everyone to see. Thankfully, the rest of the players were focused on the ball.

But what would happen when they looked up?

"Defective ball," the referee announced. "Back-up ball in play."

I *have to get out of this game.* One thing was clear to her: that feeling of being in control was nothing but an illusion. A joke.

After a quick glance at her hands—her fingernails were fine, thankfully—Gabriella jogged toward her coach.

"Rivera. What's up?" he asked.

"I'm sick," she said breathlessly, staring at the ground, just in case she had *nahual* eyes. "I've gotta sit the rest of this one out."

"But—" he began.

"Sorry!" Gabriella said in a strangled voice. Then she took off running for the locker room. Gabriella crashed through the doors and locked herself in a bathroom stall, where she closed her eyes and counted backward. When she reached *one*, she opened her eyes and looked down. The *nahual* claws were gone. The only traces of them were ten small holes in her cleats.

Gabriella laughed with relief, the sound echoing strangely off the metal lockers and tile walls. *It's okay, she told herself. You are in control. There's nothing to worry about. Splash some water on your face, and get back out there.*

Gabriella opened the door, headed for the sinks, and turned on the faucet. She glanced at herself in the mirror.

Two blazing cat's eyes stared back.

No. Gabriella's heart started pounding. *But I counted—and my claws changed—*

So why hadn't her eyes?

You've got to get control of yourself, Gabriella thought as she gripped the sides of the sink for support. *Focus. Focus. Breathe. Ten . . . nine . . .*

But she couldn't wait. She didn't have the patience. She opened her eyes.

Her *nahual* eyes.

What if I can't change them back? Gabriella thought in a panic. *What if they stay like this—forever?*

Her thoughts spiraled out of control.

The rest of her teammates would think—no, they would *know*—that she was a freak. But that wasn't all.

Everyone would know that she was a cheater.

Because that was the truth, wasn't it? Somewhere, deep inside, Gabriella had to admit that she'd known all along she was using her *nahual* powers on the field. Even if she didn't mean to; even if it had all been subconscious—or even an accident—that didn't really matter, did it?

Cheating was cheating, after all.

And maybe this was the price she would have to pay—halfway transformed, half human, half . . . not. Her shame shining from her eyes, for the whole world to see.

Her eyes smarting with tears, Gabriella blinked rapidly, stared down, and wondered, *Can jaguars cry?*

She'd never heard of such a thing. No. Crying—with real tears and everything—was decidedly human.

When Gabriella looked up again, there they were: her old, familiar brown eyes. Just like Maritza. Just like Ma. Just like Tía Rosa.

I'm back, Gabriella thought with joy as she grinned at her reflection. *I'm back!*

And just in time, too—for at that moment, the locker room door banged open.

"*Mija?*" her mother's voice echoed off the tiles. "You in here?"

"Yeah," Gabriella called and then cleared her throat.

Tía Rosa, Maritza, and Ma hurried up to her. Ma placed her hands on Gabriella's flushed cheeks. "Sweetheart, what happened?" she asked urgently. "Are you sick?"

"I'm okay," Gabriella replied—and she meant it. "I got a little lightheaded on the field. You know. Woozy."

Ma shook her head. "All that adrenaline," she said, wrapping her arm across Gabriella's shoulders. "You girls were running so hard in the sun. It's a wonder you didn't pass out!"

Tía Rosa, though, was watching Gabriella carefully. "Adrenaline, huh?" she asked, as if she didn't quite believe her. "You feeling better now, *mija*?"

"Way better," Gabriella assured her, though she couldn't quite meet Tía Rosa's eyes.

"I don't want you playing anymore today," Ma said firmly. "Enough is enough. You need some rest, some time out of the sun—"

"Yeah, of course," Gabriella said. "The game's probably about over by now, anyway."

"Let's get you home," Tía Rosa said, patting Gabriella's back. "Go ahead and change. We'll run home and get the car."

"It's only a couple blocks," Gabriella protested. "I can walk. I'm fine."

But one look from Ma silenced her protests.

Once her family had left, Gabriella opened her locker and pulled out her street clothes. Suddenly, her phone buzzed, clattering across the locker's metal shelf.

Six missed texts! Gabriella thought as she glanced at the screen. And all of them from Fiona.

EMERGENCY! MEET AT THE GYM NOW!

Chapter 6
THE COMPENDIUM

Fiona hurried into the Ancillary Gym, cradling her backpack as Darren closed the door behind her. They were immediately swarmed by the First Four: Ms. Therian; Mack's grandfather, Akira Kimura; Yara Moreno; and Sefu Badawi.

"Are you all right?" Ms. Therian demanded urgently. "What happened?"

Yara held up a wrinkled hand. "Dorina, let the children catch their breath," she said. "It's obvious they've been through something traumatic."

It is? Fiona wondered. She noticed Mack hovering at the edge of the group, his eyes dark with worry. She tried to smile reassuringly, but just then—

Bang!

The door flew open again, making everyone jump. But it was only Gabriella, out of breath from her dash across the school. She was still wearing her soccer uniform. *The big game,* Fiona remembered suddenly. It looked like Gabriella had left right in the middle of it.

"Sorry I'm late," Gabriella said. "I came as soon as I got your text. What's going on?"

"Come," Mr. Kimura said to Fiona and Darren. "Sit. Tell us what happened."

"We went to the library at New Brighton University," Fiona began. "Darren and I wanted to research Circe's Compass. We thought there might be information in the rare books collection, where we found the book that told us about the Horn of Power."

"But there were these guys," Darren spoke for the first time since they'd arrived. "I thought they were students at first. They were searching for something—and they were getting frustrated. . . ."

"I was getting frustrated too," Fiona chimed in. "The digital record seemed incomplete. I couldn't find a single entry about Circe's Compass *or* the Horn of Power—no matter how I searched. So I decided to take a look at the actual book we'd seen before."

Fiona paused, her hands hovering over her backpack. But she didn't open it. Not yet.

"I was right about the digital record," she said. "Because in the book—the real, physical book—there was so much more."

"The letters," Darren said, shaking his head as if he still couldn't believe it. "They swirled around, switched places, formed entirely new words."

"Whoa," Mack breathed.

"That sounds like something from a movie," Gabriella said, an edge of disbelief in her voice.

But Fiona was noticing something else—a glance, just a half second, that passed between Mr. Kimura and Ms. Therian.

"You can see for yourself," Fiona said suddenly, reaching into her backpack. Everyone watched in total silence as she unwrapped her *selkie* cloak to reveal, at last, the massive tome. Fiona placed it in Ms. Therian's hands, but Yara recognized it first.

"*The Compendium!*" she gasped.

"I never thought I'd lay eyes on it again," Sefu marveled, shaking his head.

But Mr. Kimura began to laugh. "I knew it was out there somewhere," he said. "And to think, this whole time, it was so close, hidden away in a college library."

"Jiichan, what are you talking about?" Mack finally spoke up, asking the question on all the kids' minds.

"It's not *The Compendium*," Fiona added. "This book is called *Traditions of Otherworldly Beings*."

"A clever title, but a fake one," Mr. Kimura told her. He held out his hands, palms up, and turned to Ms. Therian. "May I, Dorina?"

"Of course," she replied, passing the book to him.

"*The Compendium*," he began. "A precious resource for Changers. A living book. It contains our history— *all* our history, all these many thousands of years. Maps. Relics. Family trees. Lost lore. Hideaways. Secrets. They are all in here, carefully guarded. As you have already discovered, Fiona and Darren, *The Compendium* decides who can read it. Not the other way around."

"Well, it let *me* read it," Fiona said, her voice filled with wonder. "It showed us where Circe's Compass is—on a ship that sank in 1792, right off the coast of Middletown. We could go and get it tomorrow!"

Gabriella, Mack, and the First Four started talking at once, but Darren's voice carried above the rest.

"Those guys at the computer," Darren said. "Jack, Bram, and . . . Evan."

Everyone turned to look at him.

"They *knew* about this book," he continued. "I'm sure of it. They were desperate to get their hands on it."

"Did they threaten you?" asked Sefu.

"Well . . . ," Fiona began.

"Not exactly," Darren admitted. "They were kind of, well, menacing, I guess. It was like we could *feel* their— their intentions."

"They tried to look friendly, but their eyes were wrong," Fiona explained.

"What did they do to you?" Ms. Therian asked; her voice had a hard edge.

Darren stared at the floor. "One of them—it looked like he was getting ready to attack us and steal the book . . . there was a glow to his hands . . . so I shot a lightning bolt," he said. "I didn't mean to—well, I did—but it all happened so fast, and all I knew was that we had to escape."

There was a long silence.

"You did the right thing," Ms. Therian finally said. "Your safety is always of the utmost importance, but you must be careful in the future. Your training has barely begun, and your magic should only be used in emergencies."

"The lightning didn't hurt them. They chased us through campus."

"They were working for Auden Ironbound, weren't they?" Fiona asked. "Trying to find Circe's Compass, and us, too."

"We have to assume so," Sefu answered. "Auden's servants are too close for my liking. Think of it—*The Compendium* in the hands of Auden Ironbound."

"You worry too much," Yara chided him. "*The Compendium* can protect itself. It has defenses that not even the most powerful warlock can crack."

"We hope," Sefu muttered darkly. "But let us not forget that the book was lost when the warlocks attacked and burned the safe house at Tareth. With the way it conceals itself, it can just as easily be lost again. But *The Compendium* aside, what about the children? You cannot deny that they were in danger today. Auden Ironbound is like a wounded animal—and one must *never* corner a wounded animal."

"It seems the *children* can take care of themselves," Yara shot back. "I remember you were quite capable as a youngling, Sefu. Be careful that you do not underestimate them."

"I think we can all agree that Dorina is teaching them well," Mr. Kimura spoke up suddenly. "They were our first line of defense against the Horn of Power."

"And Auden still has the Horn," Yara added. "They are the only ones immune to its call."

"I don't like this," Ms. Therian said. "It's not right. We should put ourselves at risk first and foremost—not them. Never them."

"Do not let your affection cloud your judgment," Mr. Kimura said gently. "I have full confidence in your tutelage, Dorina. Remember why we are here. Remember what we were born to do."

"No, Akira," Sefu said firmly. "I have lived many centuries. Their lives have just begun. I may be an old man, but I know my place in the great circle. We must protect them at all costs."

"We are *all* bound to protect our cause!" Yara exclaimed. "Young and old united against whatever danger the dark powers deliver to us."

Then all the First Four were talking at once, their raised voices echoing off the walls of the Ancillary Gym.

No, Fiona thought, remembering what Ms. Therian had told them before the battle for Willow Cove. *Auden Ironbound wants this. He wants us distracted—and if we're arguing with one another, that's even better.*

She noticed then how tense Darren was, sitting beside her. His fingers lit up with crackling sparks, but he didn't seem to notice as he stared at the First Four, worry written all over his face.

This has to stop, Fiona said. And no one was more surprised than Fiona herself when she spoke.

"Excuse me," she said. Then louder: "Excuse me!"

All eyes turned to her.

"Do we get a say?" she asked, astonished by her boldness. Was it possible that *she* was challenging the First Four, the greatest Changers alive?

Apparently, it was.

For half a second, Fiona thought she saw a hint of

smile flicker over Mr. Kimura's face, but it disappeared too quickly for her to be sure.

"Of course you do," he said.

"Any decisions you make must be fully informed," Ms. Therian spoke up. "I want you to know that Auden Ironbound is angry. Without a doubt, he is determined to have his revenge. He is perhaps even more dangerous after defeat than he was before."

For the first time in her life, though, Fiona didn't need to think carefully about it. Her mind was already made up. She rose to her feet and said in a clear, steady voice, "I want to help find the compass. If Auden is after us, I want to be part of the fight to stop him."

Darren stood up too. "So do I," he said.

"And me," Mack added as he scrambled to his feet.

"Me too," Gabriella said, her cat's eyes flashing. "Otherwise, what's the point?"

All eyes turned to her.

"We all have this—this—this *ability*," she said, struggling to find the right words. "I guess you could call it a gift, maybe. A challenge, definitely. But if we don't use it for good . . . why should we have it at all?"

The First Four exchanged a glance. Fiona could tell that they were discussing the matter silently among themselves, reaching a secret conclusion.

"I'm sorry," Sefu finally said. "It's just too dangerous. You need to understand that these people who came after you—they're not the bad guys in your comic books and your movies. They will *kill* you if given the chance. They will come after the people you love."

"I agree," Ms. Therian said, nodding her head. "If Auden Ironbound realizes that you have The Compendium, you're at even greater risk. And there's no doubt in my mind that his henchmen would recognize Fiona and Darren after their encounter in the library. Right now, at this very moment, they are probably working on a plan to find you—and follow you straight to Circe's Compass."

"We should assemble an outside team made up of those the warlocks wouldn't recognize," Mr. Kimura suggested. "It will take a week or so, but I think that would be the safest option."

"A *week*?" Fiona exclaimed. "But—"

"You needn't worry about the compass," Ms. Therian interrupted her. "We can take it from here."

Chapter 7
THE SECRET MISSION

Their response hit Mack harder than he'd thought. Mack, Gabriella, Darren, and Fiona had saved the Changers once before, and they could do it again. He was sure of it.

This isn't over. Mack sent the thought to his friends. *I'll talk to Jiichan. Maybe he'll be able to convince the others.*

But that was easier said than done.

"There's nothing I can do," Jiichan said as they pulled into the driveway at home. "The First Four put everything to a vote, and the vote was that you are not ready."

"But we are!" Mack cried. "You have to know that.

And besides, when we defeated Auden on the beach, we were definitely not ready, but we still did it!"

"I understand that you are frustrated," Jiichan said calmly. "But the First Four's decision is final. Now, I am expecting company at any moment and will need your help to prepare."

"Who's coming over?" Mack asked.

"His name is Miles Campagna," Jiichan replied.

Mack scrunched up his face. He'd never heard of Miles Campagna before—and Mack was pretty sure he knew all of Jiichan's friends. "Who is—" he began.

"I'm sorry, Makoto," Jiichan interrupted him. "But I am really quite behind. Please tidy those papers on the table, make some tea for Miles, and keep him company in the kitchen. I will join you both as soon as I can."

"Yes, Jiichan," Mack said, stifling a sigh.

After Mack filled the teakettle, he started to stack some papers and folders that Jiichan had left on the table. *This is ridiculous,* Mack thought in frustration. *Circe's Compass is out there—we know where it is!—but Jiichan wants me stuck in the house, getting ready for a tea party. Why are we wasting time? We need to get the compass now!*

Suddenly, a label on one of the folders caught his eye. It read: MILES CAMPAGNA/AATXE.

Mack's fingers hovered over the folder; hesitated. He wasn't a snoop. He wasn't the kind of person who enjoyed going through somebody else's stuff. And yet, that word—"*aatxe*"—caught Mack's attention and wouldn't let go.

Mack sneaked a look at the door, but there was no sign of Jiichan. *Just a peek*, he promised himself, already feeling guilty.

Then he opened the folder.

MILES CAMPAGNA

Age: 26

Changer form: *aatxe*

Mack sucked in his breath sharply. *Miles is a Changer!* he thought in excitement. He didn't even know what an *aatxe* was (or how to pronounce it for that matter), but he was dying to find out. Mack turned back to read more, but the next words on the page stopped him.

Occupation: assistant manager at the Middletown
Marina

This changes everything, Mack thought. If Miles worked at the Middletown Marina, if he would help Mack and his friends rent a boat, maybe, and pilot it out to the site of the shipwreck . . .

The plan was forming so fast in Mack's head that he didn't even notice the teakettle's high-pitched whistle as steam billowed from its spout. The only thing that could shatter Mack's thoughts was a knock—sharp, loud, insistent—at the back door.

Mack was so startled that he jumped, dropping the file. As the pages scattered across the floor, Mack panicked. "Hang on!" he hollered to the visitor, who was still knocking, as he ducked under the table and grabbed the stray sheets of paper and then shoved them back into the folder.

Mack hurried across the room and checked the peephole to find a tall, lanky guy standing on the doorstep. He had rough stubble on his cheeks and a shiny metal stud in his ear. His dark hair was all messy and tousled—not like he'd tried to style it that way, but like he just didn't have time. Mack recognized him from his picture in the file and opened the door.

"Are you Miles?" Mack asked.

"Are you *Mack*?" the guy said. He reached out, grabbed Mack's hand, and started shaking it. "You—what you did on the beach—"

Miles took a quick glance over his shoulder. Mack immediately held the door open wider. "Come in," he said.

"It was incredible!" Miles continued as soon as he was safely in the Kimuras' kitchen. "Everybody's still talking about it—you know that, right?"

Mack shook his head. "Jii—um, my grandfather—he doesn't tell me much."

Miles flashed him a crooked kind of smile. "Well, you and your buddies are pretty much celebrities," he said. "I forgot how young Changers don't really get out much beyond your training unit, do you? But trust me, when you're a little older, and out on your own, there's this whole network of Changers who will have your back and be there for you, no matter what."

"Cool," Mack replied. He didn't really know what else to say.

"You saved us all, you know—you and your friends," Miles continued. "Nobody saw it coming—that warlock mess. I'm in your debt, man. If I can ever do you a favor . . . um, you going to get that teakettle?"

"Right! Tea!" Mack exclaimed. He dashed over to the stove and turned off the burner to silence the shrieking kettle. "Do you want some tea? We have, um, green tea, and white tea with ginger . . ."

"White tea with ginger, for sure," Miles replied. "Thanks. I've been on the ocean all day, and let me tell you, it's a lot colder out there than it is on land."

"What were you doing? Surfing?" Mack asked, even though he was pretty sure he already knew the answer.

"Boating, actually," Miles replied. "I work at the Middletown Marina. We do a few glass-bottom boat tours on the weekends."

I *bet you do*, Mack thought as he made the tea, all the while trying to get up the courage to ask for that favor Miles had offered. Mack knew that he couldn't just blurt it out. . . . He needed to be subtle, to figure out the right way to ask. But the clock was ticking; Jiichan could appear in the kitchen at any moment—and then, Mack knew, his chance would be lost.

"So . . . what kind of Changer are you?" Mack asked as he brought two steaming cups of tea over to the table.

"*Aatxe*," Miles replied, a hint of pride in his voice. "The bull."

"So I *did* see you on the beach!" Mack exclaimed. "You have reddish brown fur, right?"

Miles raised an eyebrow and then nodded. "I can't believe you remember. I barely remember anything that went down. What was that, your first mission?"

"Yeah," Mack said. *This is it*, he told himself. *You're not going to get a better chance.* "So that favor you mentioned? I was wondering . . . would you take my friends and me out sometime, on one of those boats?"

Miles shrugged. "Sure, no problem. You just have to bring an adult along, since you're not eighteen yet."

"That's the thing," Mack said. "This would be more like a . . . mission than a tour. If you know what I mean."

Miles leaned back in his chair and gave Mack a long look. "Go on."

"I don't think it would take long," Mack said in a rush. "We know exactly where we need to go. My grandfather wouldn't even miss me. We're talking, like, an hour. Two, at the most."

"I don't know, man," Miles said. "Is this going to be dangerous? Because your grandfather really should—"

"No! Not dangerous at all!" Mack assured him. "And if there's any sign of trouble, we'll call the whole thing off. I promise."

"That seems fair." Miles finally gave in. "I mean, I take people out on these tours every day. They're pretty tame. And I *do* owe you one."

"Thank you!" Mack exclaimed. "Can we go tomorrow?"

Miles scrolled through the calendar on his phone. "Tomorrow's no good, and we're closed on Monday," he said. "Tuesday?"

"Sure," Mack said at once. "We'll be there right after school."

That crooked smile crossed Miles's face again as he made a note in his phone. "You want a speedboat, maybe?" he suggested. "That glass-bottom boat is pretty slow."

"A speedboat would be perfect," Mack said.

"I'll take care of it," Miles promised. "Hey, do you mind making another cup of tea?"

"I would be happy to," Jiichan said as he entered the kitchen. His eyes flickered over to the table. "There's my file! I've been looking for it this whole time! Mack, thank you for entertaining Miles while I was occupied."

Mack could tell that was his cue to leave. "Anytime, Jiichan," he said. He could barely hide his smile as he hurried from the room. The mission was *on*—and he couldn't wait to tell his friends.

Mack somehow managed to keep quiet about Miles until the end of Changers class on Monday, when Ms. Therian left to check inventory in the storage lockers. Then he told Darren, Fiona, and Gabriella all about his plan.

"I met this Changer, Miles," he began in a hurried whisper. "He's a friend of Jiichan's, and get this—he works at the Middletown Marina. He says he can take us out on one of the speedboats *tomorrow*! We can go get Circe's Compass after all!"

"He would do that for us?" Fiona asked in disbelief.

Mack nodded. "He feels like he owes us for saving

him from Auden Ironbound during the invasion," he explained.

Darren slowly shook his head. "You heard the First Four," he said. "They're already making plans to get Circe's Compass next week."

"Are you kidding?" Mack asked. "We can't afford to waste two whole weeks while they try to pull together some special team of outsiders to do the job!"

"Those magic-users in the library," Darren said. "You didn't see them, Mack. You didn't see their eyes. They for sure know what Fiona and I look like. Remember what Ms. Therian said? They'll be watching for us."

Mack waved his hand in the air. "Don't let the First Four make you doubt what you can do," he said. "You and Fiona totally defeated those weak magic-users before. If you have to, you can do it again—and Gabriella and I will be there too. And Miles! He can turn into a bull!"

"As surprising as this might sound, I'm with Mack," Fiona said bluntly. "I think it's worth the risk. If we can secure the compass, we can prove to the First Four that we're ready for real missions *and* make sure that all young Changers like us are safe."

Mack turned to Gabriella. "What do you think?"

She shrugged. "You guys already know I'm in," she said. "My feelings haven't changed since Saturday. I think it's time we show the First Four what we can really do."

"Okay. Fine. I'm in too," Darren said with a sigh. "But how are we going to get to the marina?"

"I have it all figured out," Mack said. "There's a movie theater across the street from the Middletown Marina. Jiichan already said he could drive us there. He'll think we're watching a movie, which gives us, like, two hours. It's going to work out perfectly!"

"I hope you're right," Darren said.

"Everything will be fine," Mack assured him. "*Especially* when we have Circe's Compass, safe and sound."

The bell rang then, so Mack grabbed his backpack and slung it over his shoulder.

"Mack! Wait up!" Gabriella called to him. "Do you have Comics Club today?"

"Yeah. You want to come?" asked Mack.

"I thought I might check it out—if that's okay," she

replied. "I have a few minutes before practice starts."

"That's awesome. I think you'll like it," Mack said as they walked across the length of the school. "We're mostly just working on our comics for the art show. You should definitely do one."

"I don't know much about comics. . . . Actually, I don't know *anything* about them," Gabriella said. "I wouldn't know where to begin."

"That's okay," Mack assured her as they walked into the meeting. Mack's best friend Joel nodded to Mack from the other side of the room. "You'll do great. And I can help—not that you'll need it."

Mack found some extra charcoal and a stack of handouts about panel sizes, lettering, and other techniques for creating a comic book. Then he pulled two desks together at the back of the room, so he and Gabriella could talk.

"I wanted to return this," Gabriella whispered, reaching into her backpack for *The Emerald Wildcat, Volume 1.* "Thanks so much for letting me borrow it. I really loved it."

"Anytime! I brought these in for you, too, just in case

you were still interested," Mack replied as he searched in his own backpack and then presented her with issues two, three, and four. Gabriella's whole face lit up when she saw them.

"Awesome!" she exclaimed. Then she lowered her voice. "To read about a real *nahual*—doing good in the real world—it's so . . ."

"Inspiring?" Mack guessed.

"Comforting," Gabriella said. She glanced down for a moment. "Do you realize how *in control* the Emerald Wildcat must've been? Nobody knew who she was— even though she was totally public about her *nahual* abilities! And using her *nahual* powers in her human form so naturally. I mean, that is *amazing*!"

Mack wasn't sure what to say. "Listen . . . about last Friday," he began. "I feel really bad. I didn't mean to call you out in front of Ms. Therian. I'm sorry if I got you in trouble."

Gabriella shrugged. "It's not your fault I can't control it," she whispered. "Besides, it's probably better that Ms. Therian knows. She's watching me, you know, pretty closely. And part of me wonders if . . ."

"What?" Mack asked after Gabriella's voice trailed off.

Gabriella looked away. "If I'm the reason why they didn't want us to finish out the mission to get the compass," she confessed.

"Whoa," Mack said—then immediately wished he could take it back when he saw how miserable Gabriella looked. "Is it really that serious?"

"Part of me feels like Ms. Therian thinks so and worries that she told the rest of the First Four," she replied.

"That's ridiculous!" Mack said. "We need you! You're the strongest person in our group."

Gabriella tried to smile. "Thanks," she said. "I'm going to try my hardest. It's like the line dividing my human self and my *nahual* self is all blurry. Sometimes I start transforming, and the worst part is—the worst part is—"

Gabriella's voice dropped so low that Mack had to lean in close to hear her.

"I don't even realize it."

Mack remembered how frustrating it had been when he couldn't figure out how to transform. This, though, seemed immeasurably different.

It seemed terrifying.

"The truth is, I need help. If I knew another *nahual*—someone who understands what it's like or could teach me how to control my transformations—"

At last, Mack knew how he could help. "Ask Ms. Therian!" he said eagerly. "The First Four must know an adult *nahual* somewhere in the world. You know they'd connect you and—"

"Come on, Mack. If I told Ms. Therian *everything*, she'll assume I can't handle going on *any* missions, and all I'll do is hold you guys back. We'll still be doing kiddie stuff when we're forty! She'll think I'm totally out of control. If I can't help—if I can't *fight*—then seriously, what is the *point*?"

"But—" Mack began.

Gabriella kept talking. "I'm just going to be extremely careful," she continued. "I think I've already identified some triggers—like getting really upset or carried away—like with soccer. And besides, I think I already know an adult *nahual*." She tapped the cover of *The Emerald Wildcat, Volume 2*. "Remember? My mom!"

"That would definitely help," he agreed. "But . . . if you're wrong . . ."

Gabriella sighed heavily. "That's the problem," she said. "I can't just go up to my mom and ask her straight out. Because if I *am* wrong—"

"Have you tried asking Ms. Therian? She could—"

"I tried. She said she isn't allowed to reveal other Changers. It's a security thing."

Mack drummed his fingers on the desk, deep in thought. "Maybe I can help. I'll do whatever I can to help you figure out the Emerald Wildcat's true identity."

"Thanks," Gabriella said. Then she glanced at her phone. "Oh man! Practice starts in, like, three minutes!"

Mack glanced at Gabriella's paper, where she'd drawn an excellent outline of the Emerald Wildcat's mask. "Hey, that's really good," he said.

"Thanks," Gabriella repeated. "For everything."

Then she shoved the sketch into her backpack and hurried from the room.

Chapter 8
A Drink For Warriors

Despite running all the way to the locker room and changing into her practice uniform as fast as she could, Gabriella was still late. The entire team was already running drills by the time Gabriella reached the field—and Coach Connors was *not* happy with her. Even though they had (narrowly) won the game on Saturday, she could tell Coach was upset with her disappearing act in the second half.

"Rivera! Get out there!" Coach Connors barked as Gabriella jogged up to him.

"Sorry I'm late," she began, but Coach just blew his whistle—loud—and pointed toward the field.

Things only got worse from there.

It turned out that concentrating on keeping her *nahual* powers under control meant that Gabriella was really distracted—to say the least. For the first time since she'd joined the team, Gabriella was last in drills, trailing behind all the other girls. A sense of unease crept over her as she tried to keep up. *Have my powers been there all along—even before I knew about them?* she wondered. *Maybe I never was a sports superstar. Maybe I've always been a cheater, and I never even realized it.*

Thweeeeet!

Coach Connors's whistle pierced Gabriella's thoughts.

"Rivera! Look alive!" he shouted from the sidelines.

Gabriella automatically reached for a new burst of speed—then stopped herself. *You're on your own,* she thought. *No* nahual *speed. No* nahual *strength. Just you, for once.*

"Pick up the pace, Rivera!" Coach yelled.

I can't, Gabriella thought miserably. She already knew what would happen if she gave in. She could feel her *nahual* powers pulsing just beneath her skin. How could she concentrate on stupid soccer drills when it took everything she had to keep her Changer abilities under control?

Practice dragged on like that for another agonizing hour until, at last, Gabriella heard the sound she'd been waiting for: two short blasts on the whistle. *Finally,* she thought with relief as she walked over to Coach Connors for the postpractice rundown.

But Coach Connors wasn't done with them yet.

"That practice was a disaster," he said bluntly. "I have no idea how you could play so well on Saturday and then turn into such a disgrace by Monday. Now, listen up: I want you all to go home. Eat a good dinner. Get some rest tonight. Because tomorrow, you're going to train twice as hard to make up for today."

As the girls moved toward the locker room, Coach asked Gabriella to wait. "I don't know why you were holding back out there, Rivera," he said. "But we *both* know you can do better."

"I know," Gabriella whispered.

"I can see it in your eyes," Coach continued. "You're as disappointed in your performance today as I am. Don't start phoning it in. Lazy habits are hard to break."

That's when tears filled Gabriella's eyes—but for once, she didn't mind. It felt good to let it out.

"Go on, get changed," Coach Connors said, putting a reassuring hand on her shoulder. "You'll do better tomorrow."

But Gabriella wasn't convinced. As she trudged back to the locker room, worries flooded her mind. *If my talent isn't me,* she thought, *if everything I have ever achieved in sports is just because of my powers—which I can barely control—how can I keep playing? I don't have the ability on my own . . . and I can't run the risk of undergoing a transformation and destroying everything.*

The other girls in the locker room were pretty subdued too, so at least Gabriella didn't have to try to keep up with the usual chatter and laughter. But when she walked out of the locker room and saw Ma waiting for her, Gabriella couldn't hold her emotions inside any longer. She took one look at her mother and burst into tears.

"*Mija!*" Ma exclaimed as she wrapped Gabriella in a hug. "What's wrong?"

Gabriella had to bite her tongue to keep from spilling *everything.* It was so tempting—and if she couldn't trust her own mom, then who in the world *could* she trust?

Remember the secret, Gabriella thought firmly. *You made*

a promise to Ms. Therian and your friends. Telling could put them in danger. You've got to keep the secret. No matter what.

"I just had a rough day," Gabriella murmured, her voice muffled as she leaned her head against Ma's shoulder. "It's—I'm so glad to see you."

Ma brushed Gabriella's hair away from her face and then kissed her cheek. "Come on," she said as she reached for Gabriella's backpack. "I know exactly what you need."

Gabriella and her mom didn't talk much on the short walk home, which was just how Gabriella wanted it. She was still so tempted to say something—to spill *everything*—and that, Gabriella knew, would be the biggest mistake she could make.

When they got home, Tía Rosa took one look at Gabriella's tear-streaked face and gave her an enormous hug.

"Do you want to talk about it?" she asked.

Gabriella shook her head.

Ma gave Gabriella a long look. "But you know you can, right?" she asked. "Whatever it is—anything at all—you can talk to your *mami*. Or Tía Rosa."

"I know," Gabriella said as she tried to force a smile.

Maybe soon, she thought. *If I can find a way to figure out if you're a* nahual *like me.*

Ma scanned Gabriella's face for another moment and then marched over to the cupboard.

"What are you doing, Isabel?" asked Tía Rosa.

"Oh, I'm sure you can figure it out," Ma replied as she got out the vanilla and unsweetened chocolate. Then she rummaged around in the fridge for a bright green chili pepper.

"*Xocolatl!*" Gabriella and Tía Rosa exclaimed at the same time. The spicy hot chocolate was an old family tradition—the perfect remedy for chilly weather, rainy afternoons, and bad days.

Ma just smiled as she began to slice the chili pepper into round, green rings. She boiled the pepper slices in a pot of water, and the sharp, spicy scent made Gabriella's nose tickle. After Ma strained out the peppers and seeds, she returned the spiced water to the pan and stirred in some vanilla.

"Sugar?" Ma asked, glancing at Gabriella. Whenever Ma had made *xocolatl* in the past, she'd added plenty of sugar to temper the bitterness of the chocolate and the spiciness of the peppers.

"Sugar?" scoffed Tía Rosa. "In *xocolatl*?"

"The girls like it a little sweet," Ma replied. "You know it's too strong for children, Rosa. Even Mami used to add honey when we were little."

"No sugar," Gabriella spoke up. "Not this time."

"Yes!" Tía Rosa cheered. "That's my brave girl. *Xocolatl* is a sacred drink. It's your heritage."

"Our ancestors, the Aztecs, used to drink *xocolatl* for strength and courage," Ma said, whisking cocoa into the spicy water until it frothed and foamed.

Ma poured the mixture into three heavy mugs. Tía Rosa brought one over to Gabriella and winked as she placed it in front of her. "It will give you strength and courage too," she whispered.

Gabriella smiled as she brought the mug to her lips and took a sip. Without sugar, *xocolatl* tasted completely different. Bitter and fiery, it burned Gabriella's throat when she swallowed. But even though it wasn't the most delicious drink Gabriella had ever tasted, there was something about it that made her want more. Just one taste made her feel calm, strong, and clear-eyed. As she took a second sip, Gabriella understood why a warrior would crave *xocolatl*.

Because right now, with Ma and Tía Rosa by her

side and Aztec blood in her veins, Gabriella felt strong enough to face anything.

After dinner Gabriella retreated to her room to start her homework. She did her best work—Ma would accept no less, and Gabriella knew that if her grades started to slip, Ma would yank her out of soccer faster than she could blink. And then Coach Connors would be *really* mad.

But the moment Gabriella finished her last math problem, she reached for the packet she'd gotten at Comics Club. She'd never been that interested in art, but all afternoon she'd been longing to keep drawing the Emerald Wildcat. In the privacy of her bedroom, Gabriella could even get out the mask and look at it while she drew, instead of trying to re-create it from memory.

As soon as the outlines were done, Gabriella shaded in the mask with a bright-green pencil. But it wasn't enough. The mask she'd drawn was missing something—the ethereal, green glimmer that made the Emerald Wildcat's real mask so alluring.

Gabriella frowned. Then, entirely on impulse, she smudged a little iridescent green eye shadow onto her drawing to make the mask shimmer.

Better, she thought. *Now on to the rest.*

The minutes ticked away while Gabriella sketched, erased, sketched again, and shaded. The blank nothingness of the page was soon transformed. It wasn't a great drawing—maybe it wasn't even a good drawing—but there was no mistaking it: The Emerald Wildcat was taking form, right on Gabriella's paper.

Even after she said good night to her family, Gabriella was glued to the page. She glanced guiltily at the door as she slipped into bed. *Ma won't care if I draw a little longer*, she thought, stifling a yawn.

The pencil in her hand made her feel as strong as the *xocolatl*. She imagined what it would be like to feel this way at her next soccer game . . . to run without fear, to score without worry. *I am in control of my powers*, she thought contentedly as she slipped into sleep, her sketchbook still in hand.

And suddenly, Gabriella wasn't just in control of her powers. She was *using* them. *I am a* nahual! Gabriella thought with pride as she raced down the field with her jaguar speed. When she kicked the ball, it soared into the net like a missile. Again and again and again, she ran, she kicked, she scored. If the Emerald Wildcat—whoever she was—could own her powers, then so could Gabriella.

The game ended, but not before Gabriella scored one last goal. She threw back her head, laughing in triumph as she punched her fist high into the air. All her teammates swarmed around her, calling her name as they lifted her up.

They love me the way I am, Gabriella thought joyfully. *Just like everyone loved the Emerald Wildcat.*

Then Gabriella felt a strange, rippling sensation at the top of her head. *Wait*, she thought frantically.

But it was too late.

Two tufted ears.

Two glowing cat's eyes.

A long, swishing tail.

And a body, head to toe, covered in jet-black fur.

The transformation happened so fast, it left Gabriella breathless. There was a price to pay, she realized numbly, for using her powers. There was no halfway point, no middle ground. The joke, of course, was that she'd ever thought she was in control. Her careless mistake couldn't have been further from the truth.

And that was the last thought Gabriella had before she tumbled to the ground and landed with a hard thud.

She looked up from the muddy field into the hard, hateful eyes of her teammates. They had transformed too—from supportive friends to jeering enemies.

"Cheater!" came a voice.

"Freak! Freak!" Trisha screeched, pointing a long finger at her. Soon, everyone else had joined in too.

Gabriella tried to breathe; tried to count. But all she could manage was wrapping her long tail around herself and hanging her head in shame.

Then it got worse.

Trisha—or Abby or Lauren or Josie—reached out and grabbed a handful of Gabriella's silky fur. Grabbed and yanked hard, leaving a bald patch in her sleek coat. When someone else did the same, Gabriella realized that she had to get away. She wasn't safe anymore.

Then again, was she ever?

Gabriella's *nahual* speed came to her rescue then as she leaped away from her teammates and bounded over to the sidelines, where, to her surprise, Mack, Darren, and Fiona were waiting.

"Please," she gasped. "Help me."

But her friends just stood there, staring at her.

"How could you?" Mack asked.

"Everyone knows now," Darren said, glancing wildly around. "Everyone knows!"

"I'm sorry!" Gabriella moaned. "I never meant—"

A thick, choking cloud swirled up from the ground, cloaking them in mist.

"He's coming," Fiona cried in a panic. "Auden Ironbound is coming! No—he's *here!*"

That's when Gabriella awoke, her face wet with tears that had soaked her drawing of the Emerald Wildcat. It took a moment—several moments, actually—for her to realize that it had all been a dream. And that meant Gabriella's secret was still safe . . . for now.

Gabriella picked up her drawing and stared at it. Even though it was hopelessly smudged, she could still see the shimmer of the Emerald Wildcat's mask through the tearstains.

"Who are you?" she whispered.

Then she crumpled up her ruined drawing and threw it into the trash.

Chapter 9
The Seafarer

Fiona held on to the side of the boat and breathed in deeply. The sea spray on her face was more than just refreshing; it was tempting. In just minutes, Fiona knew, the boat would approach the site of the ship-wreck and she'd be able to transform into a *selkie* at last. It had been so long since she'd swum freely in the great blue ocean. The saltwater pool in the Ancillary Gym was fine for practice—but it definitely wasn't the same.

"So . . . do we have a Plan B?" Darren asked suddenly.

Everyone turned to look at him—except for Fiona, who kept her eyes on the horizon.

"Why do we need a Plan B when Plan A hasn't failed yet?" asked Mack.

That got Fiona's attention. "Plan A is *not* going to fail!" she exclaimed. She'd been up half the night memorizing everything she could about the wreck of the *Seafarer* and poring over the enchanted pages of *The Compendium*. Fiona was determined to make their mission a success—and when she was determined to succeed, practically nothing could stand in her way.

"Sorry. That came out wrong," Mack quickly apologized. "I meant, obviously, Fiona's going to rock this, so why do we even need a Plan B?"

Fiona laughed. "Don't oversell it, Mack," she said.

"Like, here's the thing," Darren began. "How come we're so sure that Circe's Compass is still down there? There are always divers scouting around shipwrecks, looking for treasure or cool stuff. Wouldn't it have been found—or looted—long ago?"

Everyone turned to Fiona. Darren had a good point; luckily, Fiona had a good answer.

"Remember what Ms. Therian said last week? Circe's Compass is protected by Changer magic," she explained.

"Only a Changer can see the chest it's in; it will be invisible to everyone else. The *Seafarer* might've been picked clean over the years; there might be nothing left—but if Circe's Compass was on that ship, it must still be there!"

Fiona glanced back out to sea. "Unless a Changer took it—which is always a possibility, I suppose. But if a Changer had found it, I feel like *The Compendium* wouldn't have shown us the site of the shipwreck. The book . . . it keeps track of things."

"Almost there," Gabriella spoke up suddenly. She'd been studying the map that Fiona had copied from *The Compendium.*

Fiona hugged her backpack as Miles cut the engine. "Is it time?" she asked eagerly.

Miles glanced around. "Yeah," he finally replied. "This is it. Are you sure you kids know what you're doing? I was there last month. I know everything you guys did for us against Auden Ironbound, but—"

"Look," Mack said. "We may be kids, but we're a lot tougher than you think."

Miles looked unsure, but it was too late to turn back now.

Fiona picked up her cloak, and Darren stood beside her, cracking his knuckles. Already tiny sparks of electricity were forming at his fingertips.

"You want to go?" Fiona asked.

Darren grinned. "Ladies first," he replied.

Fiona nodded and then wrapped the cloak across her shoulders with a flourish. She took one last breath as a girl—as a human—before she spun and transformed into a seal.

It was as easy as that.

With big, dark eyes, Fiona in her seal form watched as the blinding bolt of lightning materialized, signifying Darren's transformation. In his *impundulu* form, he stretched his long wings, displaying all his shimmering white-tipped feathers, and then folded them neatly against his back.

Good luck with the lookout, Fiona thought to him.

You too, he replied. *Not that you'll need it.*

Then Fiona plunged into the cold, murky waters. As a human she would've been freezing cold, unable to see a thing.

But as a seal? The experience was completely

different. The shafts of sunlight that filtered through the water provided more than enough illumination for Fiona to clearly navigate. She'd already figured out how to use the choppy waves to her advantage, propelling herself forward with their momentum. And the bone-deep chill of the water? In her *selkie* form, Fiona didn't even notice it.

Fiona was so tempted to swim freely, darting over and under the waves. But now was not the time. *Would it ever be the time,* she wondered, *or will I only be allowed in the ocean on missions?* No, now was the time to stay focused, as always. To find Circe's Compass and keep it safe.

Fiona plunged down, down, down into the depths. All the breathing exercises she'd been working on in Changers class were really paying off; somehow, her lungs felt full of clear, oxygen-rich air, even though she'd already been underwater for minutes.

Suddenly, Fiona heard it—an achingly lovely melody, a sound that only seemed possible beneath the sea. It echoed through the water, growing more and more beautiful until it made Fiona's heart surge with joy.

Where did it come from? What could it be? The sound made her want to breech the water and swim out to the horizon, to that magical place where the sun kissed the sea. Where, Fiona realized, she would find her kind: *selkies*.

Is *that the song of the* selkies? she wondered. Are *they singing right now, somewhere near? Are they singing to* me?

Fiona shook her head and dove deeper, though every part of her longed to turn around. Whether or not the *selkies* were trying to reach her, Fiona couldn't allow herself to be distracted. Not when she was so close to reaching the wreck of the *Seafarer* . . . and hopefully Circe's Compass too.

Because she *was* close, Fiona realized all of a sudden. There, on the ocean floor, was a shadow. More than a shadow—a dark form, protruding from the sand.

The Seafarer, Fiona thought. As she swam nearer, the ship seemed to change size and shape. Was the water distorting it? Or was it enchanted, just like Circe's Compass, and appearing only because a Changer was near?

Fiona supposed she would never know for certain.

With her strong tail, Fiona propelled herself toward the shipwreck. It was a dank, dreary place; the frame of rotting wood like a bony rib cage. There was a large hole in the hull; no doubt the reason why the ship had sank.

Fiona pushed the thought from her mind as best she could. Then she swam forward. The gaping hole was large enough that she could slip through it effortlessly. That was the easy part.

Now, Fiona thought, to find Circe's Compass.

The rotting wreck was even darker than the ocean depths, but somehow Fiona could see enough to swim through it. It was in such a state of decay that she couldn't tell one hollowed room from the next. What was she looking for, exactly? Fiona wasn't sure. But she had a feeling that Circe's Compass would reveal itself to her. That was what Ms. Therian had promised, after all.

Then, at the fore of the ship, Fiona caught sight of a strange, ghostly glow. It flickered and shimmered, casting a strange light through the rippling waters. Fiona the girl might've been afraid to approach it.

But Fiona the selkie was fearless.

She approached the chest eagerly, knowing already

that she would find Circe's Compass inside. *Incredible*, Fiona marveled. *Circe's Compass, lost, waiting for all these years . . . and I'll be the one to find it. My hands, the first hands to touch it since it was stashed in this chest for safekeeping, hundreds of years ago.*

Just the thought made Fiona swim faster.

The chest wasn't locked, which made it easy for Fiona to push the lid open. The beams that spilled from it were so bright that Fiona had to look away. Then, as the light began to dim, she peered inside, ready to grab Circe's Compass and swim back to the speedboat.

There was just one problem.

The chest was empty.

No, Fiona thought, first shocked and then confused. She was *certain* that the chest had glowed with Changer magic.

So where was the compass?

Could it have fallen from the chest when the ship sank? Fiona wondered, glancing warily from side to side.

Slowly, Fiona turned around—just in time to see the most horrifying thing in her life. Not the ghostly skeletons of the lost crew, picked clean by hungry fish, but the *Seafarer's* rotted mast, all 180 feet of it, tumbling in her direction. Underwater, it didn't make a sound.

Fiona darted away just in time. A second later, the heavy mast landed on the chest, smashing it to splinters. Billions of tiny bubbles raced up to the surface of the water. For a moment, Fiona couldn't see a thing.

Then the bubbles cleared, and Fiona saw a pearl-gray dolphin zipping away from her, a glowing object— Circe's Compass no doubt—held in its mouth.

Fiona knew at once that it was no ordinary dolphin. No, it had to be a Changer, sent here to find the compass, just like Fiona.

Could it be Yara? Fiona thought. Yara was an *encantado*, a dolphin Changer. Did the First Four know they were here?

Wait! Fiona thought desperately. *Please—wait!*

But the dolphin—whoever it was—ignored her plea. It swam faster and faster, until Circe's Compass was just a faint, glowing beacon, bobbing in the distance.

Chapter 10
THE WARLOCKS & THE TRAITOR

The air was changing.

Darren could feel it right away, probably before anybody else—any human, that is. There was a particular prickling to his feathers, as if they were standing on end. It wasn't just the wind, which was suddenly stronger, or the unexpected dampness in the air. There was something more—something that put Darren on edge. The warning of a storm, perhaps? *But the forecast was clear,* Darren thought, remembering how he'd checked the weather on his phone that very morning.

He arced back around, circling the speedboat. The sun was starting to set, but with his perfect *impundulu* vision, he could easily see Mack; Gabriella; and their driver, Miles. All was fine onboard. So Darren shifted focus, scanning the choppy waves for Fiona.

There was no sign of the *selkie's* gray pelt.

She's still below, with the ship, Darren thought. He wondered, briefly, how long Fiona could hold her breath underwater and then wished he'd paid more attention to her training times in Changers class. She had easily been underwater for twenty minutes now. Even a *selkie* needed to breathe fresh air, Darren suspected. Even a *selkie* needed oxygen.

Anxiety crept over Darren as he watched the water for Fiona. He wouldn't relax until he saw her, safe and sound, with his own eyes.

How long can it take to search a shipwreck? Darren thought. He honestly had no idea. If he tried to send a message to Fiona, would she even be able to receive it underwater? Or did they need to be able to see each other, like usual?

Darren thought it was worth a try, anyway.

Hey, he thought, picturing Fiona in her *selkie* form, slicing through the white-capped waves below. *Surface when you can. Let us know you're okay down there.*

Darren waited.

And waited.

But there was no sign of her.

Several yards from the boat, he noticed a strange turbulence in the water. The waves looked especially foamy, and there was—Darren focused with his *impundulu* eyes—something bobbing on them.

Driftwood?

Maybe, Darren thought, but that prickling feeling intensified.

Something was wrong.

Darren flew down, beating his powerful wings against the wind. His eyes moved back and forth, back and forth, desperately searching for a sign that Fiona was okay.

Suddenly, she appeared, using all her strength to breach the surface of the water, and then gracefully diving back into its depths. Darren started to grin. *Okay, Fiona,* he thought. *You got our attention. Now where is the compass?*

To Darren's surprise, Fiona didn't swim back toward the boat.

Instead, she was heading in the opposite direction.

That's when Darren realized that Fiona wasn't leaping from the water in triumph. No, it was a signal that they should follow her.

And that's exactly what he did.

Darren was flying so low that he could hear the rumble of the speedboat's engine as Miles gunned it. Darren knew without even looking that Miles had turned the boat around and was now directing it in pursuit of Fiona.

But Darren, with his strong *impundulu* wings, was faster.

Soon, he was flying directly above Fiona, soaring easily through the air as she . . . led them toward shore? Darren frowned. There was no sign that she'd found Circe's Compass . . . so why did she want them at the beach?

Darren glanced toward the shore and saw three figures standing there, staring anxiously at the ocean. He recognized them at once.

The one in the middle was wearing a red New Brighton University hat.

Those guys from the library! Darren thought. *What—*

how—why? His questions were forming faster than he could process them.

Does Fiona know they're here?

How did she figure it out from underwater?

Why is she leading us to them?

Then the most astonishing thing happened—and Darren suddenly understood everything.

If he hadn't seen it with his own eyes, Darren hardly would've believed it: A sleek dolphin, glistening in the water, leaped high in a graceful arc—higher than Darren ever would've guessed a dolphin could leap. But as the creature began its descent, something strange happened. A rippling mist crept over the dolphin from nose to tail, leaving in its wake a woman wearing a silver wetsuit. She effortlessly bodysurfed one of the waves toward the shore.

A *Changer!* Darren thought in amazement. But who was she—and what was she doing here? Had she joined Fiona underwater to help?

A bright flash suddenly caught Darren's eye, and that's when he noticed the prize proudly clutched in the unknown Changer's hand: a gleaming, golden orb.

The sun wasn't shining; the cloud cover was thick now, and yet Circe's Compass continued to wink and gleam as though lit from within.

He knew in a second that this mysterious Changer had somehow managed to nab Circe's Compass. *No wonder Fiona was swimming so frantically,* Darren thought as he flew overhead. At that moment, Fiona surfaced and pulled herself onto the beach. He'd never seen her transform so fast—she was just a blur as she whipped off her *selkie* cloak and dashed after the mysterious woman on her own two legs.

Not far away, Miles anchored the speedboat. The group headed up the shore and into the woods as a series of fast flashes—one, two, three—told Darren that Mack, Gabriella, and even Miles had transformed.

The unknown Changer knew they were after her, of course. And if she was working with the three guys from New Brighton University, there was no doubt in Darren's mind that she was on the wrong side.

Why? Darren thought in anger. *Why would you betray your own kind?* Below, he watched her make a beeline for the warlocks.

Crack!

The lightning bolt slid from his talons effortlessly. It hit between the warlocks and the unknown Changer, turning the miniscule grains of sand under her feet into glass. She jumped, startled, and then glanced at the sky. Her eyes narrowed when she spotted Darren. He simply flung another lightning bolt between them to prevent her from reaching the others.

This time, though, his aim was off, and the lightning bolt landed several feet away. The unknown Changer laughed. She shook her head, sending water droplets flying from her long, wet hair.

"Hand it over!" Evan, the guy in the red hat, yelled at her as Darren prepared to launch another bolt of lightning. He pointed toward the shore, where a jaguar, a bull, and a fox were now running toward them.

"There's no way I'm letting you take credit for this one! I'll give it to Jasper myself!" the unknown Changer shouted as Evan lunged for Circe's Compass. But she was too fast for him. She held it away and then took off running for the grove of stunted pine trees at the edge of the beach. Bent and broken from years of salt spray and relentless ocean winds, the pines were seriously malformed, but they provided the perfect escape route for the unknown Changer and her accomplices. Under their tangled cover, Darren couldn't see a thing that was happening from the air. All he could do was watch in dismay as his enemies disappeared, with his friends in close pursuit.

Forget this, Darren thought angrily as he glided toward the shore. If he couldn't help from overhead—as an *impundulu*—then he would just have to follow Fiona's lead and fight in his human form.

The sounds of the battle within the grove were nearly wiped out by the roar of the sea, but Darren had a better plan for finding everyone: following the unusual tracks—fox and jaguar and bull—that had been left in the damp sand. Even the cushiony moss that grew beneath the pines was shredded by claw and hoof marks. It didn't take Darren long to reach the scene of the battle. Though it wasn't as epic as their fight against Auden Ironbound and his army of hypnotized Changers, it was no less intense. Perhaps the danger was even *greater* now, in this hand-to-hand, face-to-face combat against three desperate warlocks on the side of evil—and a Changer who was willing to betray her own kind.

Darren pressed himself behind a tree and sized up the scene. His greatest strength right now, he knew, was to stay invisible. To avoid charging into the fight without a solid plan in place.

Off to the side, Miles lay, knocked out. Mack and Gabriella were battling the magic-users in a cloud of shifting light. Their sharp claws were deflecting curses, which ricocheted into tree trunks, scarring them with dark, smoldering wounds. It was nothing short of awe-inspiring to watch, and for a moment—just a moment—Darren lost track of everything: time, space, even his own self.

"Darren!"

It was Fiona's voice ringing through the clearing.

But . . . where was Fiona?

Darren opened his mouth to call back to her but then stopped. He still had the element of surprise on his side. Fiona must be battling the betrayer, the unknown Changer, both of them in their human forms on this unforgiving ground away from the sea.

Darren dropped to the ground and crawled, as low as he could, toward the next tree trunk. That's when he spotted them, tangled in a desperate fight for Circe's Compass. The unknown Changer was trying to hold it high out of Fiona's grasp, but Fiona almost had it . . .

Zing!

The lightning took everyone by surprise—even Darren himself. He stared at his fingers in astonishment.

The battle paused in a moment of miraculous stillness as everyone else turned to stare too. Someone moved, or maybe just flinched; then Mack growled—a long, low sound of menace—and lunged at Gabriella's opponent.

One of the magic-users stumbled back, unsteady on his feet.

Gabriella seized the opportunity to move on. Her *nahual* ears pressed back against her head, and she entered an attack posture—head down, muscles taut. Then she charged, with all her might, at the unknown Changer.

The betrayer didn't see Gabriella coming. The unknown Changer took the hit full force, flying through the air and landing, face-first, in the mud. With her quick cat reflexes, Gabriella dived forward and seized Circe's Compass with her sharp teeth.

Somehow in that moment, her eyes met Darren's, and even more astonishingly, they shared a small smile. And Darren knew that Gabriella was thinking exactly what he was:

Finally.

A swirl, a blinding flash: Mack took his human form, towering over the injured magic-users and the unknown Changer.

"It's over," he declared. "Surrender to us."

For a moment, Darren thought they actually might. The one called Bram was bleeding badly; even Evan, their leader, was casting around desperately, trying to figure out a way to escape.

Never corner a wounded animal. Darren remembered Sefu's words suddenly.

The next thing he knew, Darren was flat on his back, fighting for breath, as prickly pine needles rained down on him.

Chapter II
STUCK

Mack couldn't move. He couldn't breathe. Every cell in his body was screaming out for oxygen, and all he could do was lie there, staring stupidly at the trees and their ugly needles, which scraped against the eyes he couldn't even blink. Mack could hear Miles in his *aatxe* form chasing off the warlocks, but the sound was dull, as though there was cotton in his ears.

Then, suddenly, like the sun burning away a stubborn fog, the paralysis spell lifted. Mack tried to take a deep breath but ended up coughing and choking uncontrollably.

He wasn't the only one. Around him, Gabriella and Darren and Fiona were struggling too. The fight for breath was almost worse than the paralysis. Before, at least, it had been out of his control. But now? He was trying as hard as he could . . . and failing.

"Breathe," Miles commanded them as he came running back to the clearing. "Breathe deeply. You'll all be fine—but breathe, now, do it! Even if it's hard. Even if it hurts. *Breathe.*"

Mack focused on Miles's voice until, little by little, his lungs stopped seizing and relaxed into slow and steady respiration. *Breathe in. Breathe out,* he told himself. *Breathe in. Breathe out.* Soon he felt strong enough to sit up—and start asking questions.

Miles held out his hand for Mack. "What was *that*?" Miles asked fervently, his eyes blazing. "Those guys— and that lady—where did they go? And the— Was that really . . ."

Mack held up his hand. "I'm afraid that's classified," he said. Somewhere behind him he heard Darren snort.

Miles raised an eyebrow. "Is everyone all right?"

"Yes," Darren and Fiona said at the same time.

"Gabriella?" Mack asked. The *nahual* nodded and then padded across the clearing on broad paws. She dropped the compass's case near the others and transformed back into her human form.

"Looks like everyone's fine," Mack said, picking up the case. "Let's check it out!"

The kids crowded around Mack while he opened the compass's case. If its gold metal had glowed before, it *blazed* now, emitting beams of light in a wild spectrum of color. Mack didn't know much about precious jewels, but he had a feeling that those were real rubies, diamonds, emeralds, and sapphires studding the surface of the compass.

Everyone watched as the compass's arrow moved in a slow, purposeful circle, pointing first at Miles, then Mack to Fiona to Darren, and finally to Gabriella.

"Awesome," Mack whispered, his face beaming.

"It's beautiful," Fiona marveled. "I mean, I was impressed when I saw it underwater—but this is about a million times more amazing."

Darren pointed at the compass's surface. "What's wrong with the arrow?" he asked. "It's stuck."

Fiona frowned. "Perhaps it's picking up on a stronger signal from a nearby Changer," she mused.

Everyone tensed at once, remembering the unknown Changer. The betrayer. Was she still near—lying in wait—ready to attack?

But when Mack and the others looked warily in the direction that the arrow was pointing, all they saw was Gabriella.

Well, no.

Not exactly Gabriella.

Who they saw there—or *what* they saw there—was not really Gabriella at all.

Part girl, part *nahual*, her golden cat's eyes glimmered with panic as she stared at her human hands, from which cruel, unforgiving claws protruded. Two plush, velvety cat ears stuck up comically from her head, and a long, furry tail snaked behind her in the dirt.

"Oh no," Mack whispered before he could stop himself.

"I—I'm stuck," Gabriella said miserably, her voice choked and halting. "I—I—I—"

Miles rubbed his temples. "Okay. Okay," he said. "Look, Gabriella, um, stay calm. This happened to a guy I know when we were in training. You're going to be fine."

"Do your counting thing!" Fiona suggested.

"Okay," Gabriella said as she took a deep breath. The clearing was completely still except for Gabriella's small voice as she dutifully counted backward. By the time she reached five, Mack realized that he was holding his breath. And by the time she reached one . . .

Nothing happened.

"Do it again," Miles said, so firmly that Mack realized—for the first time—that he was worried. *Really* worried.

Still nothing.

"I have an idea," Darren spoke up. "Why don't you transform fully into a jaguar and then back into your human form? Maybe it will be like pushing a reset button."

"Okay," Gabriella said eagerly, nodding her head. "Okay. I'll try it."

Seconds later, the jet-black *nahual* stared at them and then blinked her golden eyes.

After Gabriella tried to transform back, those golden eyes were still staring.

"It didn't work!" Gabriella cried.

"That's it," Miles said. "I'm going to call your grandfather, Mack."

"No!" Mack exclaimed. "We can handle this. Gabriella, why don't you try counting backward again—"

"Come on, man," Miles said, not unkindly. "Secret mission or no, this has gone too far. Those warlocks meant business, and there's no way we can take Gabriella back to the marina like this. If somebody saw her—"

"Miles is right, Mack," Fiona spoke up. She put her hand on Gabriella's shoulder. "It's okay to ask for help when we need it—and right now, we *definitely* need it."

"Stay here," Miles told them, holding his cell phone in the air trying to get reception. "I mean it. Nobody leave. I'll be back as soon as I can."

There was a heavy silence as Miles walked away from the clearing. Then Gabriella burst into loud, choking sobs.

"What am I going to do?" she wept. "What if I stay this way—forever? I can't go home like this."

No one knew how to comfort their friend, who was suffering so deeply.

"I'm being punished," Gabriella said. "For using my

powers in soccer, for being a cheater and a liar, for all those wins that were unfairly won. I'm not human—not like this. At best I can be an animal, I guess. And at worst—a *freak!*"

"Don't say that!" Fiona exclaimed. "You're not a freak. N*one* of us are."

"And you're not a cheater," Darren said firmly. "Your abilities are natural! You were born with them!"

"They're part of who you are," added Mack. "It would be lying to cover them up. What would your teammates think if they knew you were holding back? Wouldn't that be worse?"

"Nothing could be worse than this," Gabriella replied, holding up her claws for all to see.

"You just need help," Darren told her.

"What if no one can help me?" Gabriella shot back. "What then?"

That gave Mack an idea. He held up Circe's Compass and dangled it before Gabriella's face. "Then maybe," he began, "you'll need to help yourself."

It was all Mack had to say; Darren and Fiona looked confused, but Gabriella understood perfectly.

"You think—" she began.

"I *know*," Mack interrupted her. "Go. Find the Emerald Wildcat. You've said all along she could help you. Now give her the chance."

"Hold on a second," Darren spoke up. "What if those magic jerks are still out there? Or that dolphin lady?"

"You think they're a match for Gabriella?" Mack scoffed. "Even if they ganged up on her, Gabriella could escape and leave them all in the dust. Nobody's faster."

"That's true," Fiona said. She reached out and squeezed Gabriella's arm. "You be safe out there, okay?"

"She'll be fine," Mack declared. "Besides, we all know she's the best fighter in the group."

"Thank you," Gabriella whispered. Without another word, she took Circe's Compass and hung it around her neck. It dangled there, gleaming and winking as if it had a secret.

Then Gabriella transformed, fully, into her *nahual* form and charged away from the clearing.

Chapter 12
The Emerald Wildcat

It wasn't luck that allowed Gabriella to race home to Willow Cove as a jaguar without being seen. In her *nahual* form, Gabriella was able to run miles in minutes, so fast that she was a blur.

Gabriella ducked into her house and transformed silently as soon as the door closed behind her. A quick glance in the entryway mirror told her that she was still partially changed—*Oh, those ears!* she thought in dismay. She couldn't even bear to think about her tail. . . .

Gabriella forced herself to take a deep breath. *You're home now,* she reminded herself. *Safe.* The smell of chocolate was heavy in the air, and someone in the kitchen was singing in Spanish. A thrill of hope spiraled inside Gabriella, making her dizzy. *Ma,* she thought, placing her hand on the doorframe to steady herself. This was it: the moment of truth. Circe's Compass would reveal everything that Gabriella had longed to know.

With trembling hands, Gabriella opened the compass. The arrow was spinning in wild circles, casting a sparkling rainbow light across her face as Gabriella watched. Then, suddenly, the arrow stopped, quivering as it pointed to the kitchen.

I *knew it!* Gabriella thought joyfully. Her mother—her own *mother*—was the Emerald Wildcat! A wide smile spread across Gabriella's face, even as she rubbed her tickly nose. There was *xocolatl* simmering on the stove, no doubt about that; the heady mixture of chocolate and spice filled the air. Somehow Ma had known, just like she always did, that Gabriella needed her. Maybe that was part of *her nahual* powers.

A *family recipe,* Gabriella remembered. A *drink for warriors.*

Gabriella burst into the kitchen. "Ma, I need—" she began.

But that wasn't Ma at the stove.

It was Tía Rosa.

Rosa turned around, spoon in hand, with a smile that vanished the minute she saw Gabriella's face.

"*Chica valerosa*," she whispered as she held out her arms. "*Such* a brave girl. Come here, *mija*."

Brave? Gabriella thought numbly. She didn't feel very brave as she stood there, staring with disbelief at her aunt. She felt muddled and mixed-up, confused and, well, *wrong*. In her uncertainty, Gabriella's tail flicked involuntarily, brushing against her legs.

If Ma's *not the Emerald Wildcat*, Gabriella thought, *then . . .*

Tía Rosa crossed the kitchen and wrapped Gabriella in a strong hug. "Everything's going to be okay," she whispered near her ear. "You've been strong for so long, *mija*, but you don't have to be strong by yourself anymore. I'm here."

Gabriella started to cry again—but this time, the tears that cascaded down her face were from relief. Tía Rosa patted Gabriella's hand as she led her over to the kitchen table. She poured each of them a steaming mug of *xocolatl* and then sat across from Gabriella.

"Ask me anything," Tía Rosa declared, holding her hands palms-up. "I'm an open book. Your mother and Maritza won't be home until suppertime. It's just you and me."

"So *you're* the Emerald Wildcat?" Gabriella blurted out.

A sly smile crept across Tía Rosa's face. "I was," she said. "But that's a story for another time."

"I've been trying to figure out the Emerald Wildcat's real identity," Gabriella said as she showed Circe's Compass to her aunt. "I thought she was the only one who could help me. I—I found the mask. In the attic. So I thought it was Ma. But . . . I guess I was wrong."

"I really need to get the rest of my junk out of your attic," Tía Rosa said. She touched Circe's Compass with the tip of her finger. "I'm sorry, *mija*. You shouldn't have needed this to find me. I should've reached out to you sooner."

Gabriella paused to sip the spicy, bitter *xocolatl*. "Is Ma a *nahual* too? Like us?" she finally asked, not wanting to give up that last shred of hope.

Tía Rosa shook her head. "I'm afraid not. But you—I always had a funny feeling about you. And when I saw you playing soccer on Saturday, well, it was clear that you'd come into your powers."

"Come into my powers?" Gabriella repeated. "I can't even control them." She flexed her fingers to extend her claws. "What am I going to do?"

To Gabriella's surprise, Tía Rosa didn't look even a little concerned. "This? This is nothing," she scoffed, laughing in a friendly way that immediately made Gabriella feel better. "When I was thirteen, I had whiskers for a *week*! A whole week! Your *abuelita*—yes, she's a *nahual* too—couldn't stop laughing. I didn't leave my room for *days*!"

Gabriella tried to picture Tía Rosa as a teenager with long cat whiskers—and just the thought made her start laughing too.

"It's so common for young *nahuals* to have trouble with their transformations," Tía Rosa continued. "But you *will* master it, *mija*. I promise."

"You really think so?" Gabriella asked, daring to hope.

"I know so," Tía Rosa replied, tapping her chest. "In my heart. Besides, all that extra effort I put in to mastering my transformations really paid off in the end. That's how I could become the Emerald Wildcat, with the ability to channel my *nahual* powers while still in my human form. A little coaching from me, and you'll be the same. I'm sure of it."

"A crime-fighting superhero?" Gabriella asked.

"A girl in control of her powers—and her destiny," Tía Rosa corrected. "But for now, let's focus on getting you back into your own skin."

"I'll do anything you say," Gabriella said. "I've tried everything I could think of. Even counting doesn't work."

"Sit back and relax," Tía Rosa said. "Let go of all the stress, all the worries. All the fear. Let it melt away. Good. That's good. Already your face looks more relaxed, *mija*. Now, focus on your breathing. Slow and steady. Good girl."

The soothing sound of Tía Rosa's voice, calm and familiar, washed over Gabriella. In moments, she felt calmer than she had since school started.

"I want you to concentrate on the tips of your toes," Tía Rosa continued. "Flex and release—flex and release. Then your heels . . . your ankles . . . your knees . . . one part at a time, until you reach the top of your head. And this time, I'll do the counting. Ten . . . nine . . . eight . . ."

When Tía Rosa reached "one," Gabriella exhaled. She knew without even checking that her transformation was complete.

And she was right.

"Good girl," Tía Rosa said proudly. "I knew you could do it."

"It was easy with your help," Gabriella said. "But how will I do it when I'm on my own?"

"Practice," Tía Rosa replied. "Practice, practice, practice. You'll get it. And until you do, I'll be here to help."

Gabriella smiled at her aunt. *It really is going to be okay,* she told herself—and at last, she believed it.

BANG!

At that moment, the back door flew open so hard that the glass window in it shattered.

The three warlocks from the forest stood in the doorway. The one in the red hat had a nasty sneer on his face, but it was his eyes that really unsettled Gabriella: dark, hollow, empty.

"Just give us the compass," he said with a snicker. "And nobody has to get hurt."

Chapter 13
FIGHT OR FLIGHT

Tía Rosa and Gabriella were on their feet in an instant. "Get out of here, Gabriella," Tía Rosa ordered.

"No," Gabriella argued. "I can fight."

The three magic-users had a good laugh at that, which filled Gabriella with rage. *Hold on to the anger*, she reminded herself as her power surged. *Use it.*

"You'll stay out of the way—and stay safe!" Tía Rosa shot back. And those were her last words to Gabriella before she spun and landed on the table in a crouching position. Gabriella pressed herself against the wall and watched in astonishment. She'd never seen anything like it—here was her aunt, her beloved *tía* Rosa whom she'd known all her life, still very much in her human skin—but moving, growling, *thinking* like a *nahual*.

She's not Tía Rosa anymore, Gabriella suddenly realized. *She's the Emerald Wildcat.*

And what a wonder it was to see the Emerald Wildcat in action; all that *nahual* power so masterfully contained in one human body. She moved with unspeakable grace as she leaped through the air, knocking out one of the guys with a sharp kick to the jaw. Then Gabriella caught a glimpse of a tail, and when Tía Rosa reared back and lifted her arms, Gabriella noticed thick sharp claws jutting from her fingertips.

Swipe!

Tía Rosa's claws flashed through the air, leaving four long, red streaks on the other guy's face. He fell to his knees, howling in pain as he clutched his cheek, then disappeared in a gust of smoke.

Two down in less than a minute, Gabriella marveled.

But the third warlock, Evan, was ready to fight back. He muttered something unintelligible under his breath as a flash of red lit up his eyes. A harsh tremor passed through the kitchen, rattling every cup and plate in the cupboards. Even the *xocolatl* mugs tipped over, spilling onto the floor.

"Kid stuff," Tía Rosa scoffed, her voice a half growl.

"I've heard about you," he replied. "The Emerald Wildcat. The humans sure thought you were something special . . . but I'm not impressed."

"You think I care?" Tía Rosa asked as she bounded to the top of the cupboard. Her long tail flicked back and forth, like a warning. "You punks come into my *sister's* house, threaten my *niece*? You won't be leaving here without a pretty pair of magical chains."

Red light blazed in the boy's eyes. "You're washed up," he said, but Gabriella could hear the panic in his voice. "You're nothing!"

"You made a mistake siding with Auden Ironbound, but it's not too late to make it right," Tía Rosa continued. "You seem like a smart kid. Now, let me tell you how this works. You're gonna sit down, nice and slow, tell me why you trashed my sister's house and what you want from my niece. Then—"

There was no warning.

A boom.

A blinding flash.

A shimmering bubble, glowing with cold light,

enveloped Tía Rosa. She stood motionless inside it, her face contorted in an expression of pain.

"No!" Gabriella tried to scream, but she was frozen too. She could only watch in horror as Evan lunged for Circe's Compass—sitting on the table, out in the open . . .

All of a sudden, Gabriella broke the spell with a cry of rage. She knew what to do: transform at once, just like she'd tried to do before Tía Rosa had stopped her. In her *nahual* form, Gabriella could take on anyone.

She lunged forward, blocking the magic-user as he reached for Circe's Compass. Then Gabriella threw back her head and roared so loud that all the windows shattered in a glittering explosion of broken glass—and the bubble holding Tía Rosa captive burst.

Tía Rosa fell to the floor into a crumpled heap . . . and didn't move.

The sight of Tía Rosa lying there, so still, so pale . . .

And it was all *his* fault . . .

With one swift, seamless leap, Gabriella had the warlock cornered. To his credit, he had the sense to look scared as she roared again.

Gabriella. Stop, Mack's voice rang through her head.

A half-glance over her shoulder revealed a *kitsune* in the doorway. Mack. And behind him she saw Darren and Fiona, Ms. Therian and Mr. Kimura.

Gabriella shook her head and then leaned closer to the magic-user.

Come on, Gabriella, Mack urged her.

Gabriella hesitated; the anger was so hard to rein in. . . .

"She's not backing down, Akira." Ms. Therian's voice floated through the room.

"I don't think she can," he replied.

In a flash, Ms. Therian had crossed the room and locked the other unconscious warlock in glowing bonds that kept his wrists held tight. Mr. Kimura, in his *kitsune* form, leaped between Gabriella and the one who had hurt her aunt.

"Gabriella!"

That voice got her attention.

With a ferocious snarl, Gabriella backed away. Her golden cat's eyes never left the warlock's face.

Gabriella turned her head to see Tía Rosa gingerly pulling herself up.

"Gabriella. *Mija,*" Tía Rosa repeated.

Gabriella slowly blinked her cat's eyes, the pupils

dilating and constricting as she tried to focus on her aunt.

"Come back to us, brave girl. Come back."

Her transformation back to her human form had never been easier.

"Tía Rosa!" Gabriella cried as she rushed across the room to embrace her aunt. "Are you all right?"

"I will be," Tía Rosa said. "Once I get over the humiliation of that little punk warlock getting the best of me. I've never been more ashamed!"

"Forget him," Gabriella said as she helped her aunt over to a chair. "You were *amazing!*"

Tía Rosa cracked a smile. "Maybe I've still got it."

Yara and Sefu arrived then, stepping delicately over the mounds of broken glass strewn about the floor.

"It's safe," Gabriella said right away. She cupped Circe's Compass in her hands before giving it to Ms. Therian. "Circe's Compass is safe. I—I know we shouldn't have gone after it. . . ."

"We wanted to prove that we could do it," Mack said.

"That we're strong enough—" Fiona added.

"You don't need to say anything," Yara interrupted them. "We know why you did what you did."

"Miles showed us the clearing—or what is left of it—and he explained about the *encantado* who tried to steal the compass," Mr. Kimura said. He fixed each of them—Gabriella, Mack, Fiona, and Darren—with a somber stare. "And now this room . . . destroyed. You showed great courage in seeking out the compass, but you put yourselves as well as Miles and Rosa in great danger."

"We know you are powerful, but you have much still to learn about control," Ms. Therian added. "You kids are too important to lose. Next time, trust us."

"Still, perhaps I was wrong about you younglings," Sefu acknowledged. "Maybe you *are* ready for more responsibility. I would never have guessed that you could accomplish so much in just one day—finding Circe's Compass at the bottom of the sea, retrieving it, *and* protecting it from Auden Ironbound's henchmen? That's a full day for a team of advanced Changers—let alone ones so young."

Tiny Yara puffed up with pride. "I'm not surprised," she boasted. "These kids are tough as nails. Tougher than we were, even, when we were their age."

Yara, Sefu, and Mr. Kimura continued talking as they led the chained warlocks from the kitchen.

Mack, Darren, and Fiona followed.

Purple bruises were already forming on Tía Rosa's arm, but that didn't stop her from wrapping it across Gabriella's shoulders. At that moment, Gabriella didn't feel especially tough or brave or ferocious—because right now, she didn't need to be. As she leaned against Tía Rosa's shoulder, Gabriella felt—for the first time in ages—comfortable in her own skin.

She felt like herself.

And that, Gabriella realized, was perhaps the greatest power of all.

Tía Rosa kissed Gabriella's temple and then whispered into her ear, "You and me, *mija*. We're quite a team, don't you think?"

"I'm going to miss you so much when you go back to New Brighton," Gabriella said. "I don't want you to leave."

"You can't get rid of me so easily," Tía Rosa replied, her eyes twinkling. "I'll be seeing you every weekend from now on."

"Really?" asked Gabriella.

"You bet," Tía Rosa said. "I already talked to your *mami* about it. Because you and I? We've got work to do."

EPILOGUE

Normally, school was the last place Mack wanted to go on a Saturday, but on the day of the art show, he couldn't wait to get there. The gym—the regular gym—had been transformed, filled with sculptures, oil paintings, pen-and-ink drawings, and dioramas. The Comics Club had its very own table, and Mack was thrilled that his comic had the place of honor—right in the middle. He might not have gotten his superhero's face *quite* right—and some of his lines were a little more wobbly than he liked—but Mack was still plenty proud of his very first comic, *The Kitsune Tails, Episode 1: Den of Thieves.*

And he was even prouder that his own grandfather

seemed so impressed by it, flipping through the pages with a broad smile on his wrinkled face.

"Drawn from life, I see," Jiichan said as he studied a drawing of a *kitsune* on a beach.

"Just a little," Mack said.

"I have a feeling that there will be plenty of . . . inspiration in store for you," Jiichan said. "It seems clear to me that you will always be ready for adventure, whether or not adventure is ready for you."

Mack shifted uncomfortably. Something had been weighing heavily on his mind all week. It was time, he realized, to learn the truth.

"Jiichan," he began in a low voice. "I have to ask. Did Miles . . . did he get in trouble? For, uh, helping us the other day?"

Jiichan's face was calm. "Miles? In trouble?" he repeated. "Why would he be in trouble for doing what I asked him to do?"

"What *you* asked—" Mack began in confusion. But his voice broke off unexpectedly when he saw the knowing half smile on Jiichan's face. "So you knew we'd try to go on the mission anyway?"

"Yes," Jiichan said.

"And you needed somebody—Miles—to keep an eye on us," Mack finished. He stared at the floor. That realization was more disappointing than he wanted to admit, especially when Jiichan started to laugh.

"Oh, Makoto," Jiichan said, shaking his head, "you have misunderstood. Last week's battles were not won because you had an adult watching over you. No. They were won because you and your friends understood your strengths—and your limits—better than anyone else. Even the First Four. We won't forget that next time . . . though clearly one thing you lack is patience. We'll work on that."

At last, Mack looked up and met Jiichan's eyes and smiled. *Jiichan believed in us all along,* he realized as Jiichan patted him on the back and then moved on to look at the pottery display.

"Nice work, Mack," a new voice said.

Mack turned around in surprise. "Gabriella!" he exclaimed. "You're here! But what about your game?"

"It just finished," she told him. "Short and sweet . . . for the Clippers, at least. I don't think the Deerfield Divers are in a very good mood, though. Anyway, you know I wouldn't miss the world premiere of The Kitsune Tails! I can't wait to read it. And before I forget . . . this is for you."

Mack's whole face lit up when Gabriella gave him a copy of her own comic, The Continuing Adventures of the Emerald Wildcat.

"It's not nearly as good as what you and your friends in Comics Club have been doing," Gabriella said, a little embarrassed. "But I thought you might like it. Check this out—I gave the Emerald Wildcat a sidekick! The Jade Jaguar."

"Awesome!" Mack said approvingly, with a knowing smile on his face. "And speaking of the Emerald Wildcat . . ."

Gabriella leaned forward as Mack lowered his voice.

"Is that true? Your Aunt Rosa is—?" he continued.

"You know," Gabriella began. "As a matter of fact, I—"

"*Mija!* There you are!"

Mack and Gabriella turned around at the same time.

"Hey, Tía Rosa," Gabriella said. "I'd like you to meet my friend Mack. Mack, this is my *tía* Rosa. She's— pretty fantastic, actually."

Tía Rosa flashed a dazzling smile at Mack when she noticed The Continuing Adventures of the Emerald Wildcat in his hands. "Oh, I like you," she said, pointing at the comic book. "You have *very* good taste."

And then, to Mack's astonishment, Tía Rosa *winked*.

"Five minutes, *mija*," Tía Rosa said. "I'll be waiting outside."

Mack was speechless as Tía Rosa walked away. "Was—are—I mean—*seriously*?"

Gabriella just grinned.

"Oh, man! I can't even believe it! That's, like, the coolest thing ever!" Mack gushed. "And she was *right here*! Listen, do you think—maybe—she might want to take a look at The Kitsune Tails? Like one day, if she's bored, or something?"

"I'm sure she'd love it," Gabriella said as Mack gave her another copy. "I wish I could stick around, but I've got to go."

Mack glanced toward the door. "You guys have plans, huh?" he asked, sounding wistful.

"Yeah," Gabriella replied. "Tía Rosa's tutoring me in . . . phys ed. I want to be ready for whatever happens next."

"For the *Continuing Adventures*?" Mack said, holding up Gabriella's comic. He meant it as a joke, but as he and Gabriella exchanged a long glance, he knew it was the truth.

After all, their adventures were just beginning.

What challenge will the Changers face next?

Here is a sneak peek at

THE HIDDEN WORLD OF
Changers

The Power Within!

Bzzz.

Though Darren had *finally* fallen asleep, and his phone barely made any noise as it buzzed, he bolted upright in bed anyway, wide awake in an instant. Everything was blurry as he blinked his eyes, once, twice, and tried to focus on the blinding brightness of the screen so that he could read the text message. It was from his big brother, Ray, and just seeing Ray's name made Darren feel better—for a second, anyway.

> D, what's up? Just got your msg. I'm here

Darren had been waiting all night to hear back from Ray, but he couldn't tell him everything over text. Darren didn't know exactly what was going on—that was why he had texted Ray in the middle of the night, after all—but he knew that it was too important for a text message.

Darren tucked his phone in his pillowcase and tip-toed toward the door. It was still dark outside, but he glanced out the window, just in case Dad had come home in the night and he'd missed it.

But Dad's space in the driveway was still empty. In the dim glow of the streetlights, Darren could see that only Mom's car was parked there.

In the kitchen, Darren found Mom's laptop on the table. He snuck a glance over his shoulder, even though he was certain Mom was still asleep.

Darren flipped up the screen and logged into his V-chat account. To his relief, Ray was already logged on. A warm smile filled Ray's face as Darren appeared on the screen. Ever since Ray had moved out last year to start college at New Brighton University, Darren had missed him terribly. But V-chatting was almost as good as getting to hang out with Ray in person.

Almost.

"Big D!" Ray said, his smile widening as he leaned back in his chair. "Sorry I missed your text last night. My psychology midterm is this morning, so I was in the quiet room of the library to study for most of the night. So I didn't even get your text until, like, four AM. Otherwise, I would've been right on it. Anyway, what's going on?"

Darren got right to the point. "Dad didn't come home last night," he said, lowering his voice. "*Or the night before.*"

A look of surprise flickered across Ray's face for half a second; then it smoothed out, as expressionless as a mask. "Are you sure?" he asked. "Maybe Dad was really busy at work and got home after you were asleep."

Darren shook his head. "I waited up both nights," he said. "I'm serious, Ray, I really don't think he's been home in"—Darren paused as his throat tightened; he swallowed hard, then continued—"two days."